THE

FORD

FILES

Jn Clifford

JAMIE AND ALEX CLIFFORD

Alx Clifford

BY JAMIE CLIFFORD

BY ALEX CLIFFORD

ISBN: 9798335357845

JR RUTHERFORD BOOKS

Cover Design by AMC Cover Design

REVIEWS

Double Daggers

Double Daggers by James R. Clifford has placed as an Award-winning finalist in the Historical Fiction category for the National Indie Excellence Awards.

"*Double Daggers* is very strongly recommended as a complex, superbly crafted, thoroughly entertaining novel from beginning to end."

-James Cox, *Editor, Midwest Book Reviews*

Double Daggers was one of seven books selected by the American Numismatic Association as a notable and great read.

"James R. Clifford has been graced with a fertile imagination. This is one novel that will refuse to be forgotten long after it has been put to rest on one's bookshelf, as Clifford's characters linger in the readers' minds as well as his scenes that have an icy clarity to them."

-Norm Goldman, *Editor, Book Pleasures*

"History is evoked in James R. Clifford's novel of intrigue and suspense. Anyone with a love of history will thoroughly enjoy this carefully researched and splendidly told story that spans the centuries."

-Alan Caruba, Editor, *BookViews*

"If you want to read something edge-of-your-seat-engaging, historically fascinating, and really well written. This book would make wonderful book club fodder, it is well written and intriguing to the end."

–Michelle Boucher-Ladd, *FrontStreet Reviews*

"An attractive, enjoyable novel that even provokes thought in those who go for that sort of thing."

-Seabrook Wilkinson, *Charleston Mercury*

"*Double Daggers* is a fascinating story revolving around the infamous Eids of March coin. Combining history with a touch of the paranormal, Double Daggers is an original, well-crafted-and dare I say strange-story that will be enjoyed by all."

-Mayra Calvani, *co-editor, Voice In The Dark*

Ten Days To Madness

"*Ten Days To Madness* is an intriguing twist of psychological fiction. Highly Recommend."

-*Midwest Book Review*

"*Ten Days To Madness* is a fascinating story and extremely entertaining with may unexpected twists and turns. Mr. Clifford, created an exceptional psychological thriller with a paranormal Native American flare."

-*Tome Tender Book Review*

"It's a fast paced, page turning madness."

-Jeff Reichenberger, *E-Sylum*

5 Stars: "This is a great read. It is well written, with a great story . . . and some really cool twists."

-Goodreads

A Griffin In Her Desk

A Griffin In Her Desk was an Award-Winning Finalist in the Children's Fiction category for the National Indie Excellence Awards.

"A magical excursion from the classroom into the realm of monsters Greek gods and fabulous treasures."

-Virginia Barrett, National Committee for Latin

"*A Griffin In Her Desk* is creative education at its best."

-Diane Donovan, Editor, *Midwest Book Review*

"Mrs. Moneta makes the classics, ancient history, Greek mythology, and reading fun and educational, with her own magical twist."

-Kerry Wetterstrom, Publisher, *The Celator*

"What a fun story and truly wonderful way to bring ancient history, mythology and numismatics to life."

-Elizabeth Hahn, Librarian, American Numismatic Society

MORE REVIEWS, BIO AND BOOK INFORMATION CAN BE FOUND AT: WWW.JRCLIFFORD.COM

For Buckaroo Banzai
- No matter where you go, there you are.

THE FORD FILES

CHAPTER 1

KA-POW! MISSING

KA-POW! Five little letters that pack a mighty punch. And just like that, your life changes forever.

You may wonder who even dares to use KA-POW as a description anyways? Comic book geeks, sure. Action movie stars, definitely. Fifty-year-old men who shout *Eureka* when they successfully fix the drip from the kitchen sink, most certainly.

My name is Alex Ford and no, I am not a boy, despite the common misconception. It's an understandable mistake because 97.88% of all people named Alex are boys. I looked that fact up.

I'm fairly certain my parents were so dead set on having a boy they didn't spend any time compiling a girl's name list. Not very proactive or original on their part, huh?

Anyway, that day started like any typical Charleston summer morning. A sweltering heat that you could not understand unless you lived in the coastal south. A kind of stewing in the precipice of an acidic offshore afternoon with thunderstorms comparable to the heat rising from a boiling Cup of 'O Noodles.

1

I spent a good twenty minutes contemplating a move to Alaska that ended in Google searches for affordable log cabins, cheap airfares to Reykjavik, and a quick Amazon purchase of an extra bedroom fan.

I took a quick glance out my window spotting a pack of sweaty neighborhood kids riding their bikes down the street whooping it up, excited to have escaped the zoo for the summer. The trill of an ice cream truck moving through suburbia and the humming of cicadas and lawnmowers confirmed it. Summer was here and all was right with the world, aligned like rows of carpenter ants.

It was going to be the typical Charleston, South Carolina summer day: acidic and bright. And of course, as previously mentioned, hot as heck with a good chance of afternoon thunderstorms during a drive down a marsh bordered highway.

I had just graduated from high school, diploma and all, and was looking forward to a carefree summer before starting college in the fall. No calc work with many days spent at the beach. And like most teenagers I had it all mapped out, dotted cleanly in black ink. Or at least I pretended to during conversations with prying guidance counselors and well-meaning but annoying parents.

I was going to study pre-med, go to medical school and then after racking up a fortune in tuition debt become a doctor. Everything seemed cut and dry, void of any fault lines or pinpoint cracks. Streamlined. On an established footpath. Straight forward. Designated turns. Etc. Etc.

Of course, that was all pre the big KA-POW. I soon coined that as a wordplay off of the Big Bang. From nothing to everything but on a more miniscule scale.

I was ready to head out into the world for the day when I heard my dad calling for me to come down to the kitchen. I grabbed my beach bag, reading materials, sunscreen and walked downstairs.

Dad stood next to the oven with his arms crossed. The dishwasher was running. The coffee pot was full, bagels packed into the toaster. The kitchen island had a nice platter filled with butter and jelly and cream cheese. Our dog, Crazy Mazy, was happily lapping up a small puddle of melted ice biding his time until bagel crumbs began hitting the floor. All pretty normal and mundane to say the least. Like I said, all was right with the world.

I looked over at Mom seated at the kitchen table. She looked distressed. although I couldn't help but think it looked a bit forced. The toaster broke the silence shooting up two perfectly golden bagels as Dad dripped coffee down his shirt, right on cue like something out of a bad sitcom. I half expected to hear a well-timed laughter track. Mom shook her head and grabbed a bagel from the toaster, aggressively spreading blackberry jelly over it with an excessively large knife. Neither of them said a word. Silence, again, besides the droning of the dishwasher and the incessant clinking of the knife against the glass jelly jar.

"What's wrong?" I asked.

In a casual fashion, my parents informed me that my grandfather had disappeared. Vanished into thin air. No trace. Sayonara. Goodbye. Adios.

The KA-POW! moment.

In the blink of an eye my grandfather had become a shadow, dissolving like salt in a basin of warm water. A puddle evaporating. Nothingness. There wasn't anything dramatic about it. No cataclysmic shaking of the earth. Except for poof, he was gone.

The funny thing about nothingness is its ability to feel like something, as crazy as that sounds. There I stood with a bagel hanging from my mouth, cream cheese on my chin, stuffing my beach bag with half-eaten snacks from the cupboard, with the "oh, by the way, your grandfather is missing" hanging over me.

No biggie. Carry on. I could almost hear my mom say, better warn you the Cheeto Puffs are a little stale and make sure to grab a water on the way out and here are a few dollars if you want to get an ice cream on the way home.

And this my friends is how I metamorphosed from a mild mannered, well-adjusted, almost college student, and future doctor to a crazed lunatic living a life that closely resembled the wackiest episodes of the X-Files, Twin Peaks or The Twilight Zone.

An obsessive, psychotic teenage girl, toes on the edge of nothingness ghost-hunting with a flashlight and a homemade electronic magnetic field detector, which is a technical term for a ghost hunting device.

I spent the entire first day thinking Grandpa had some momentous senior "hit the ceiling" type of deal. Berserk. Haywire. Off the handle. Bananas.

He wasn't always the most level-headed type of person but there must've been a major lapse of concentration driving home or something. I mean, that made sense.

I could imagine him showing up with a crazy story about getting lost fishing or taking a wrong turn in a swamp while photographing egrets. Or maybe he went to see a rock concert with a distant Jersey-shore relative or an old buddy from his college days. It could happen, right? After all, he had disappeared for short periods of time during one of his so-called "walkabouts."

But each fabrication I told myself became less and less convincing. He was eccentric, but not bat shit crazy.

After five insane days passed, Grandpa Joe simply became the intangible ghost of a seventy-eight-year-old man who liked creamed corn a bit too much and watched old black and white films in his office. Nothing. Nada. Absolutely zero. Like he had never existed. A magic trick. I was waiting for him to appear in the doorframe and pull a limp, silk scarf from his lips or yank a rabbit out of a top hat.

The clouds block the sun, and the shadow disappears. At this point, even though no one would admit, we all knew this time was different. Unaligned. Like a wire had been snipped with kitchen shears.

Despite the odd circumstances, my parents were doing nil to nothing regarding the situation. I mean they didn't even post "Lost Grandpa" signs around the neighborhood. So, I decided to take matters into my own hands. I drove over to my grandmother's house to check in on her and ask some hard questions.

I pulled into the driveway next to Sheriff Walker's squad car. The sheriff had been a distant acquaintance of the families for decades and naturally he had taken a direct role in investigating my grandfather's disappearance. He was a squat, mustachioed man, heavy set and thick.

He had a disconcerting habit of picking stuff out of his teeth with a toothpick and spitting sunflowers seeds out of the window of his squad car. He preferred the takeout on Main Street and only listened to opera and something along the lines of a sixteenth century lute.

I got out of my car and snuck a peek inside the driver's side window of the police cruiser. A neon green Incredible Hulk lunch box sat on the front seat along with an unsecured shotgun, shells haphazardly strewn across the floorboards.

I shook my head. I don't know why, but I never particularly liked or trusted the sheriff. I suppose there was no reason for me to feel that way since he kept getting reelected. That must mean something, right?.

Call it a weird intuition but I had a feeling that there was something a little off. Perhaps it was his lunchbox, or the fact that his Southern drawl sounded like honey being squeezed through a waffle cone. That is if honey had a sound. Was he really from Charleston or was his drawl some type of a front? I don't know, maybe it was just his rigid handshakes and undercooked barbeque he always bragged about.

It was hard to explain but, let me point this out once again: What kind of a grown man travels around with an Incredible Hulk lunch box? To sum it up, he was the type of man who would use KA-POW in a day-to-day conversation.

Also, his name is Jay Walker. What kind of law enforcement official is named Jay Walker? Jay. Walker. Is that some kind of sad humor or irony or an oxymoron? This may sound like a stretch for the sake of storytelling, but I assure you his name was JAY WALKER as in someone who crosses a street in a careless or illegal manner!

Maybe his parents were just witty or shifty or lawyers who dressed like gavels for Halloween; either way I was rather skeptical of him. And I am certain you can see why.

I walked into grandma's home without knocking, a standard custom in our household. Grandma and the sheriff stood in the hallway having an animated conversation. The sheriff threw his stubby arms up in the air before sighing and flipping quickly through his notepad.

The pair finally noticed me. Grandma forced a small smile. "Oh hi, dear."

"Is everything okay?" I asked.

The sheriff didn't seem particularly happy to see me. He preferred to wear heavily starched khaki pants even in the sweltering summer with his holster shoved tightly under his gluttonous belly.

His police outfit reminded me of Deputy Fife in those old Andy Griffith reruns except Sheriff Walker always wore a black tie with an old black cowboy hat that always managed to sit askew on his bulbous head. However, his most distinguishing feature was a smarmy-looking, peppered, Salvador Dali-esque mustache.

I'm no expert on people but it is a general rule to never trust anyone who has a handlebar mustache. But isn't this just something that is commonly accepted though? Instilled from an early age like "stranger danger".

"I stopped by to give your grandmother an update," the sheriff answered, continuing to flip through his notepad while tapping a little golf cart pencil against his chin.

He finally looked up and announced, "I'm afraid there's really nothing more to report."

I took a deep breath. At least he wasn't here to inform us that they found grandpa's body in a marsh, half eaten by fiddler crabs and ravenous raccoons. I swiped a quick glance at his notepad. The page was blank.

The TV blared in the background distracting my thought process. I glanced over to the set to witness a demented-looking Godzilla sock puppet destroying a paper mâché replica of the Eifel Tower. For reasons unknown grandma's big screen TV was broadcasting a demented kids' puppet show from a crazy sci-fi channel that I didn't even know existed.

I shook my head and turned back to the sheriff who was also staring at the Godzilla carnage on TV but with a surprisingly goofy, yet evil-looking grin on his face.

"Where exactly is this investigation going?" I asked in frustration because Grandpa wasn't the kind of man easily lured off with the premise of candy. "I mean, how can a grown person just disappear off the face of the Earth?"

The sheriff forced his attention back to me, slowly twisting the ends of his "Salvador Dali" mustache.

"Trust me, this happens more than you think. Tens of thousands of people go missing every year. AWOL without any distinguishable trace. Especially at his age. They just become forgetful. Trust me, he'll turn up. Someone will notice an old man where he's not supposed to be."

"Those are people the mafia has put a bounty on, or people forced into witness protection. They choose to disappear," I huffed in response. "Seventy-Eight-year-old men who have been married for over fifty years and have no debts or a mafia hitman chasing them don't just vanish into thin air."

The sheriff looked a bit exasperated. I knew he didn't appreciate being interrogated by an almost pre-med college freshman, but this was my grandfather. A nice man. A simple man. A man with, yes, one too many Hawaii print button–downs and hunting lore, who took the time to talk to everyone in the neighborhood. This was Grandpa Joe.

Sheriff Walker sighed and twisted his moustache again. He then offered a limp, half-hearted shrug. He glanced at grandma and made a strange clicking noise in his throat.

"I promise you," he replied. "I am doing everything in my power to find some answers. As you know Joe had some unusual interests but like I've discussed with your grandmother, there is a distinct possibility he was out in a remote area taking a hike, fishing, whatever and he experienced a health issue."

"So, there still no sign of his car?" I tried to sound more docile and respectful in my questioning.

"No. Our best shot in these cases is tracking credit cards or a cell phone, but as you know he left those here, so we won't be able to ping a cell tower or track an ATM or credit card transaction."

"That's what I mean," I replied. "Doesn't that seem really odd?"

The sheriff sighed followed by a pathetic shift of his shoulders that might have been an attempt to signal the end of the conversation.

"And what about all that sand that was in his bed?" I continued.

"Honey, I'm sure the sand was nothing," grandma interjected. "You know he was always going to the beach or exploring offbeat areas."

"The soil around here is mostly sand," the sheriff interjected. "We live on the coast."

Gee, thanks for the information Mr. Wizard. What was wrong with these two? I thought. I was standing right here just a few days ago when grandma had described to the sheriff that it was so odd that she found a fine layer of sand covering the entire bed the morning he disappeared and not a little clump of sand that had haphazardly fallen out of his pajama pockets.

I was beginning to develop a feeling that they weren't telling me everything they knew. Or at the very least they were holding something back.

I glanced back at the TV. A psychotic-looking clown that would terrify the bejesus out of Stephen King was dancing around a circus stage singing a rhyme about purchasing time share condominiums in Florida. Dear god, what channel was my grandma watching? Was the station part of their bundled cable subscription?

"It was strange though. So strange. Sand," Grandma laughed a little too giggly. "All over the bed."

"I'll look into it, but I'm not so sure…"

"I know you don't think foul play was involved," I cut off the sheriff. "But we have an elderly man who completely disappears. His car is nowhere to be found. He leaves his wallet and cell phone at home, not to mention the sand in his bed. And on top of all that, and I know no one wants to discuss it, but grandpa did have some odd acquaintances. Maybe someone abducted him or something."

The sheriff made that strange clicking noise in his throat. He fumbled in his shirt pocket and pulled out a pair of mirrored Ray-Bans. He put them on, and the bluish lens made him look like he had bug eyes, like a prey mantis.

"I better get back to the station. Y'all have a good rest of your day now."

Grandma grabbed his forearm with both of her hands. "Thanks for stopping by, giving me an update. We do appreciate everything you and your deputies are doing."

The sheriff tipped his hat and left. A strange thought occurred to me as I watched the sheriff pull slowly out of the driveway then gun his squad car down the street. What in the heck did he keep in that Incredible Hulk lunchbox? A ham sandwich, shotgun shells or perhaps the fingers of criminals he had sent to prison.

I turned to grandma, "How are you doing?"

"I'm okay. It's just so disconcerting and hard to think about. I know this might sound awful, but I try to block it out of my mind as much as possible."

I went over and gave her a hug. She smelled of mothballs and sugar cookies. She squeezed me a little too tight before letting go.

"Would you mind helping me move a trunk into Grandpa's office."

"No problem."

I followed her down the hallway into their bedroom. The room was dark, with the curtains drawn, and claustrophobic. I tried not to gasp because there was an odor of wet gym socks mixed with mothballs.

Grandma pointed to the trunk. "I was going through some of his things last night and I just want to move this into his office."

I grabbed the trunk built out of old leather smattered with water stains and ancient dust. I hauled it down to Grandpa's office. My grandparents had lived in this house for over thirty-five years, but I had never once been in his office.

Sure, I had caught glimpses inside when the door was slightly ajar, but it had been one of those secret places designated as off limits without anyone ever really telling you that it was off limits. An unwritten, unspoken understanding.

"What's in the trunk?" I asked, setting it down in the middle of the office.

Like their bedroom his office smelled like mothballs (again) with a hint of mold from a forgotten corner of an old library. Grandpa's office wasn't as dark as their bedroom and sunrays filtered through cracks in the blinds, illuminating swirling dust moots floating like little galaxies.

"Oh, just photos, notes, his files. Stuff like that." Grandma sat down in grandpa's desk chair. She was a small woman, with medium whitish-grey hair who tended to wear flowery dresses that reached her ankles. Maybe because of all the stress but recently she appeared smaller than usual, concaving, hollowed out. Almost shell-like. I felt bad for her.

I looked around and it wasn't really what I had expected from a man who ran an insurance agency for over forty-five years. His office resembled a tightly controlled disaster area with files, papers, magazines and books strewn everywhere. It had some semblance of a hoarder but with more organization in the mass of chaos.

A large oak desk sat in the center of the room covered in maps and assorted papers. What looked like an otherworldly radio or old space junk sat on a table next to the desk.

"What's that?" I asked.

"A ham radio."

"I've heard of them. Real ancient things." I laughed.

Grandma smiled. "I guess you could say that; they're actually pretty neat. Kind of a combination between a radio and a CB. Grandpa talked to people and listened to amateur broadcasts from all over the world. He'd talk to fishermen from China, astronomers, a boat captain sailing in the Caspian Sea, birdwatchers in the Galapagos. It was endless but it kept him busy."

"That's cool."

I walked over to his bookshelf filled from floor to ceiling with books of every shape and size. Interestingly, there was not a single book on gardening or bridge or World War Two. His collection consisted entirely of obscure books about cults, conspiracies, UFOs, unexplained phenomena, monsters, haunted sites, unsolved mysteries etc. etc. Not the type of books you would expect seventy-eight-year-old grandfathers to have.

"Grandpa sure enjoyed some strange stuff, huh?"

She laughed. "In his younger days he was really into some offbeat things, for lack of a better term. And since he retired, well, I guess he ended up with just too much time on his hands. He became more involved but mostly reading and researching though. Humoring himself, I think."

I ran a finger across a hardback book by HP Lovecraft. "How come he never talked about all this?"

"You know how he was, reserved. He didn't really talk about those things too much. I don't think he really believed in all this stuff; it was just a form of entertainment. You know, an escape. Some men go hunting, some play golf, some drink, and some do other things, but this was what kept him occupied. I garden, you know. Saner, don't you think? My tomatoes would've been wonderful this year if not for the darn squirrels."

I smiled at her squirrel comment, then turned my attention to a giant built-in cabinet that lined an entire wall. "What's in there?"

"His research files. He called them The Ford Files."

Sounds intriguing, I thought. "Do you mind if I take a look?"

Grandma paused a bit too long before answering, "sure, help yourself. I'll make a cup of tea and heat us up some cookies."

I opened one of the filing cabinets and unlike his office there was order and the files were meticulously organized, labeled and dated. I pulled out a file dated 1973 titled Francis Marion Boo Hag Monster. Inside was a grainy black and white photo taken around dusk. There appeared to be an either a hairy man hunched over or a deformed bear walking in a swampy bog. A dozen typed pages of notes accompanied the photo.

I laughed a bit as I read the notes detailing Grandpa's investigation into the existence of the Boo Hag Swamp Monster. I knew there was no way Grandma was going to let me go through all these now and anyway it would take weeks of shuffling back and forth. I didn't have the time, I needed answers quickly.

Grandpa seemed to have slipped away like static. He was gone like the Boo Hag Monster two seconds after the picture was snapped, creeping back into a wooded marsh with nothing but the sulfuric smell of mud and footprints filling in with briny water.

I put the file back into its place and shut the cabinet. A thought dawned on me. I walked to the last cabinet on a hunch and opened it. I was right. These were his most recent files, so they were in chronological order.

As I suspected there was a method to this madness. I grabbed a large stack of the files just as grandma came back into the office. She carried a small China cup of Earl Grey and spun a sugar cube into the tea with her fingertip.

"Hey, do you mind if I take some of these to read? I promise I'll bring them back." I asked.

Grandma got that strange look on her face again. "Well, I guess it's okay," she stuttered. "If you promise to bring them back."

"Sure, no problem."

I gave her a peck on the cheek trying to get out of there before she changed her mind. She handed me a bundle of cookies wrapped in paper napkins and kissed me on the cheek.

"Say hello to your mom and dad for me."

"I will. And thanks for the cookies."

As I walked to my car, I felt a little better, even relieved. At least this was a start. Something. These files could hold some clues that might explain what had happened to him. Maybe it was just desperation at this point, or perhaps just my obsession with Sherlock Holmes but at least I was finally doing something to help find Grandpa.

I looked out at a storm brewing off of the horizon. Nasty shaped black clouds, expanding and contracting, filled the sky like tar. A hot gust of wind blew scattering a flock of crows from the front lawn. An enormous lightning bolt cracked across the sky followed by the loudest thunder boom I had ever heard. The air tingled with a whiff of electricity.

I instinctively sprinted to my car. I didn't think about it at the time but looking back, I wonder if that was the moment when the universe tried to warn me to mind my own business.

CHAPTER 2

THE 33RD PARALLEL:
THE BLOODLINE OF THE EARTH

I drove home non-withstanding a quick pitstop for an insanely overpriced café latte. I spent the entire day in my bedroom reading The Ford Files that I pilfered from Grandma.

Going through his files made me feel like a gravedigger robbing my grandfather's crypt, pillaging his age-old secrets and treasures with a heavy, foreign hand.

Let me tell you Ol' Grandpa was into some crazy stuff, but his files didn't read like an insane Unabomber's manifesto. There was eloquence, there was logic, due diligence and obviously a lot of research in his reports.

Even so, Grandpa didn't seem to fit the X-File profile. He was clean-shaven, wore crisp button downs, and always wore socks. Psychos opt for espadrilles and combat boots, right? I had never even seen him in sandals or flip-flops, and we live at the beach.

I had discovered a lead—The only appropriate conjecture I could pull from my repertoire of mystery novels and film noir screenings. I picked up my cell phone and called a friend from high school.

"Hey Sara, this is Alex how you are doing?"

"Not so good," she answered. "Huger is missing."

"Oh no, who's Huger?" I asked with alarm bells ringing. Was a serial abductor out there snatching unsuspecting Charlestonians. A beach bum psychopath with the intent on destroying the local tourism industry.

"It's my hamster," Sara answered much to my relief. "I was cleaning his cage, so I let him out in the back yard to play. You know, to let him stretch his legs and get a little exercise. I must have gotten sidetracked for a few minutes because when I went to grab him, he had disappeared. I mean where in the hell could a hamster go? His legs are like a millimeter tall, if he managed to walk ten feet that would be like one of us walking a thousand miles, right."

"I guess."

Jeez, I thought. Is she really crying about some stupid rodent with a lifespan of a couple of months at best? Still, I felt a little bad for Sara and if not Sara, then for Huger the Hamster, who more than likely was in the belly of a golden retriever or a hawk.

"S-sorry about your hamster," I continued. "The reason I called was to see if I could get your cousin's number?"

"Which one? You know I have like a thousand cousins."

I had to admit it was a stupid question. Sara's family was one of the original French Huguenots that had fled to Charleston in the late 1600's to escape religious oppression. Real colonial backwash. She had a billion relatives residing comfortably in coastal bungalows, sipping mint juleps in loose button-downs and watching sunsets from yachts while spending their inherited secret Swiss bank accounts filled with francs and gold.

"Charlie's number," I answered with a grimace because I knew I was about to get a barrage of questions.

"Charlie Parker?"

"Yes."

"Why would you want that lunatic's number?"

"I have a few questions to ask him?"

"What could you possibly want to ask him? You know, he's insane."

I knew I had to tell her something or I'd never get her off the phone. "Okay, but can you keep this between me and you?"

"Of course."

"My grandfather was kind of into some weird things and I came across Charlie's name and number in a couple of his files. It's a long shot but maybe he knows something."

There was a pause then Sara asked, "Hey, wait a second. Why are you calling me? You said you had Charlie's number."

I wanted to jump through the phone and strangle her. I didn't have time for this. "Well, like I said I came across his name. I called what I thought was his phone number, but it went straight to some strange, automated recording."

"What kind of recording?"

"It hard to describe. It started with eerie musical notes followed by a robotic sounding lady who was repeating numbers over and over again. Real horror movie kind of crap. It sounded like creepy elevator music meets the theme song from Halloween."

"Whatever, I've got to go look for Huger. I'll text you his cell number after we hang up."

"Thanks."

A few seconds later her text came across and I dialed Charlie's number.

"Yo, what's up?" A way too enthusiastic voice answered.

"Hi, Charlie, this is Alex Ford, Sara's friend. Do you have a second?"

"Alex Ford," he repeated.

"Yes."

"As in your related to the missing Joe Ford?"

"Uh, yeah. I'm his granddaughter."

"I'm kind of surprised someone from your family hasn't contacted me earlier," he replied nonchalantly.

"Why do you say that?"

"You just called me, didn't you?"

"Right," I answered realizing he had a point, and I was desperate enough to ignore his slightly condescending tone. "Could we meet? I have some of my grandfather's files and I'd like to ask you some questions. Maybe see if you have any insight or thoughts as to what might have happened to him."

There was an uncomfortably long pause before he responded, "Yeah, no problem. Like I said I was expecting someone to call eventually. Why don't you come down to my office? I'm on King Street above Subway. You know the one by Marion Square?"

"I know where it is. I'm heading down there now."

I hightailed down to his office. Real gung-ho. After finally finding a parking space (an impossible feat in the height of summer), I walked down to the Subway.

I took a rickety set of stairs next to the restaurant up to the second floor. The stairwell smelled like a mix of soggy Italian bread, meatballs and old wood. The overwhelming scent of cheap sandwiches was enough to do anyone over. Charlie Parker was one brave man.

A cheap cardboard sign posted next to his door read: CHARRLSTON INVESTIGATIONS. The whole scene was rather mediocre and, to be honest, a bit strange. I mean, he could at least invest in "more professional" curb appeal. The whole thing had a sort of 1950's detective vibe. I half-expected a man in a midnight-colored trench coat wearing a fedora hat to swing open the door with a certain sense of suaveness. Maybe even smoking an expensive Cuban cigar, the kind that only people with Boston accents could get away with.

I knocked, and the door opened almost immediately. Charlie was in his mid-twenties and not what I expected. Despite the heat, he wore faded blue jeans, a button-down shirt and loafers. His hair was cut short. He looked nothing like a crazy paranormal investigator or one of those ghost tour directors who shuffled inebriated packs of tourists through the city on Friday nights.

He gave me a wry smile. "Hey, I'm Charlie, C'mon on in."

I stepped inside his office which obviously also served as his apartment. The large studio space was open with lofty ceilings, old hardwood floors and faded brick walls. It smelled slightly less like cheap deli meat in his apartment than the stairwell.

On the far side of the loft an unmade bed doubled as office space with legal pads strewn across the mattress and an open closet stuffed with clothes and sporting equipment.

"Take a seat." He motioned to a worn, leather cracked chair that definitely had seen better days.

I sat down and heard a crunch from underneath the cushion.

"Oops, sorry about that." Charlie said sheepishly.

He motioned for me to stand up. He reached underneath the cushion and pulled out the remains of a frozen dinner with a slightly embarrassed grin.

"I get tired of Subway sandwiches, you know. I think I've tried every combination of meat, veggie, and condiments possible. Although, I do have to admit it is convenient living above a Subway."

I don't know whether it was because he stuck a frozen dinner underneath the couch cushion or the fact that the frozen dinner box contained dinosaur shaped chicken nuggets and chocolate pudding topped with sprinkles.

"Don't worry about it," I replied while sitting back down. "So how exactly did you know my grandfather?"

"We had mutual interests."

"Mutual interests" sounded like slang for stock deals or insurance claims, real Wall Street stuff, not anything that would remotely resemble the insanity woven into The Ford Files.

"So, you were both into unexplained mysteries, the supernatural . . . those sorts of things? Hah, never thought I'd be saying that in conjunction with my grandfather." I laughed a bit.

"That's not exactly the case. My research and investigations have more to do with good old-fashioned conspiracies, the supernatural, the occasional UFO and unsolved mysteries. Your grandfather was more into history and how it was related to mysticism and the metaphysical world."

"What exactly do you mean by the metaphysical world?"

"Well, metaphysics in general terms is just the study of nature and the origin of reality itself. You know, the immortal soul, the universe and the existence of a supreme being."

I was a little taken back by that tidbit and replied, "Grandpa Joe went to church every Sunday at ten. I never heard him discuss this kind of stuff."

"I don't know what to tell you. He was into the Big Picture. You know, the Grand Unified Theory that would explain everything."

"Interesting," I replied. "Was there anything recent that he was looking into that may help explain what happened to him?"

"Well, on a more local level he believed that Charleston was an "unusual" place and held great mysteries because of where were located."

"What's so unusual about our location?"

"Charleston sits on the 33rd parallel or what is referred to as the bloodline of the earth. You've never heard of that?"

"Ah, no. Should I have paid more attention in school?" I muttered sarcastically.

Charlie smiled. "No, you wouldn't have been taught anything about the 33rd parallel in school. I just thought your grandfather would have mentioned it?"

"No. He took me to the Ice Princesses or to Barney and later, baseball games."

"Yeah, well anyway. 33 is a sacred number and there have been so many major events that have occurred on the 33rd Parallel over the course of human civilization that it is almost impossible to chalk them all up to coincidence.

"Like what?"

"For starters: the birthplace of civilization began on the Euphrates and Mesopotamia Rivers in Iraq which is located on 33rd parallel. The Great Pyramid was built on the 33rd parallel in Egypt. Right here in Charleston the first shots of the Civil War were fired and in 1734 the first Grand Lodge of the Free Masons was formed. The only two atomic bombs ever detonated on cities were at Hiroshima and Nagasaki both on the 33rd parallel."

"Okay, so?"

"There's more. The 33rd parallel cuts through the Bermuda Triangle. The Roswell, New Mexico UFO Incident. JFK's assassination in Dallas. Babylon. Mount Hermon in the Book of Enoch. And the lost city of Atlantis were all on the 33rd or the bloodline of earth. And there are also some weird facts about the number 33. Like do you know the complete sequence of Human DNA is 33. There are 33 vertebrae in the human spine. Ideal sleep is 8 hours of 33.3% of 24 hours and .... "

"Hold on," I cut him off because I got the feeling that Charlie could go on forever with this if I let him. "Okay, this is all pretty interesting and cool. And I don't want to be all skeptical or whatever, but I don't have a lot of time. Like I told you on the phone I found your name with a phone number in one of my grandfather's files and uh… in light of your work, I thought you might be able to help me."

"What was the number beside my name?" Charlie asked.

"Hold on."

I pulled out the file from my bag then handed it to him. The number was circled in red by his name.

Charlie looked up from the file with a shocked expression. "Did you call this number?"

"Yes. I was trying to get ahold of you. But it was weird. First eerie music started playing then a strange, very creepy woman's voice kept repeating a series of numbers over and over again. I never actually talked to anyone."

He handed me the file back. "Listen to me, whatever you do, don't ever call that number again."

"Why?"

"Just don't. This is something your grandfather was working on when he disappeared. I don't know exactly but there is something not right about this recording and where it originates from."

"Do you think this number or recording has something to do with his disappearance?"

"I don't know but have you ever heard of a Numbers Station?"

"No."

"Well, your grandfather was into them big time. During the Cold War in the 1950's people started hearing bizarre radio messages broadcasted from ham radios. The simplest explanation was that these broadcasts were covert messages sent to spies throughout the world. They used ham radios because messages could be transmitted over exceptionally long distances, and it was impossible to break the codes. No one knows where they originated from or who was sending them."

"Grandpa did have a ham radio in his office. My grandmother said he would listen to broadcasts and such. She said it was just a hobby of his."

"I think he would have considered it more than a hobby. He was researching that some of the present-day Numbers Stations were broadcasting something entirely different than messages to spies."

"Like what?"

"He thought some of the transmissions were coming from a different frequency than ours."

"What do you mean by different frequency?"

"I guess the best way to describe it is like this: if you are listening to music on a radio and you switch channels, even though you can't hear it any longer the music is still playing on the previous channel, right?"

"I guess."

"Well, the fact is you just don't hear it anymore because the frequency has changed after the channel is switched."

"Okay, and what does that mean?"

"It's a scientific fact that humans can only hear or see things in certain frequencies or spectrums. But your grandfather thought there were other dimensions that were all around us, but we can't experience them because as humans we are hardwired to certain, specific frequencies or spectrums. He believed that some of these Numbers Stations are from different dimensions or realms of existences."

I laughed sarcastically. "Sounds like he might have lost touch with reality."

"Take a look at this." He handed me a torn-out page from a book.

"What's this?"

"It's a page from Edgar Allen Poe's short story *Gold Bug Island*. Have you ever read it?"

"I vaguely remember reading it at some point a long time ago for school."

"Makes sense. Poe's story was based in Charleston on Sullivan's Island when he was stationed at Fort Moultrie. But here's the weird part. See the code or cryptology at the bottom of the page?"

I looked down at the strange series of numbers and symbols:

> *53‡‡†305))6*;4826)4‡.)4‡);806*;48†8*
> *¶60))85;;]8*;:‡*8†83(88)5*†;46(;88*96*?;8)*
> **‡(;485);5*†2:*‡(;4956*2(5*—4)8*
> *¶8*;4069285);)6†8)4‡‡;1(‡9;48081;8:8‡*
> *1;48†85;4)485†528806*81(‡9;48;(88;4*
> *(‡?;34;48)4‡;161;:188;‡?;*

The random numbers and symbols looked like someone had fallen asleep on their keyboard creating an amalgamation of keyboard stroke gibberish.

Charlie continued, "This is the code found in Poe's *Gold Bug Island*. In the story the main character deciphers the code leading to treasure left by the pirate Captain Kidd." He paused and then asked me. "Do you recognize the code at all?"

"No."

"That phone number from your grandfather's notes that you called is a recording from a Numbers Station that broadcasts every 33rd day at 3:33 a.m. for 33 minutes before going silent for another 33 days. Then it repeats all over again. The woman saying those numbers over and over again is repeating the code found in Poe's story."

"What! That's crazy."

My cell phone rang pulling me back into a strange reality that smelled of stewing meatballs and Febreze.

"Hello," I answered.

"Alex, this is Sheriff Walker. Do you have a second?"

A knot started growing in my throat. Had they found Grandpa? And if they did, the news certainly couldn't be any good. Bile rose up in my throat.

"Yeah."

"I'm down at the Old City Jail and I was wondering if you could meet me here?"

"Sure. Is there something I need to know?"

"We found your grandpa's car."

"At the Old City Jail?"

"Yes."

"And uh, what about grandpa?" I asked, hoping I wasn't going to have to identify his body.

"No sign of him. Just his car and . . . Well, it's better if you come down."

"I'm on my way."

I stood up and grabbed my files. "C'mon," I replied to Charlie. "They found Grandpa's car at the Old City Jail."

Charlie stood apprehensively. "Really?"

"Yes, c'mon. That is, if you want too."

Charlie hopped up. "Yes, of course."

We drove over to the Old City Jail, and I parked right outside.

I looked at two octagonal towers soaring from each corner of the four-story building. The building projected a Romanesque style highlighted with thick walls, rounded arches and towers, bearing a semblance to a dilapidated fortress nestled in a deserted French hillside. In fact, the building could've been transplanted by ship from the Loire and shipped to Charleston. Its dark coloration seemed expectant, as if waiting for a group of revolutionaries to storm the gates as if it was the Bastille.

The building cast an ominous shadow and a weird feeling of déjà vu swept over me. I remembered three years ago Grandpa had picked me up for a little grandfather-granddaughter outing. I guess most "normal" grandfathers would have taken their granddaughters to Chuckie E. Cheese Pizza joint, the zoo or a RiverDogs baseball game. But not Grandpa Joe, he took me to one of Charleston's most haunted buildings—Charleston's Old City Jail.

I remember the jail smelled like musk of age and salt, as if the ghosts of executed pirates loomed behind the bars, baring their rotted teeth and scurvy-ridden gums while cackling promises that their treasure's location would die with them.

The building had been around since the early 1800's and had even housed POW's during the Civil War. Over the years dozens of prisoners were hung in the jail's courtyard but most met their ends thru the horrific conditions within the jail. There was nothing light about the place, I can tell you that.

One story in particular that Grandpa told me stood out because it was about the first female serial killer in the United States. Her name was Lavinia Fisher, and she ran an inn called The Six Mile House with her husband John. The inn was located six miles north of Charleston on a dirt trail that served as an important road for commerce at the time. A cross route for trade, the exchange of luxury spices and herbs for rice and barrels of beer.

The story goes that Lavinia was a stunningly beautiful temptress, a land siren, who lured solitary travelers back to their inn for dinner and rest. Lavinia would stir hemlock into their tea while John entertained the guest with dinner and then coffee by the fireplace.

He would stoke the fire and tell stories of palmetto tree forts and the Red Coats, of expansive starry nights and long, endless beaches.

Lavinia used expensive porcelain cups, shining like fresh snow, and carefully spread raspberry currants and marmalade and soft, whipped butter on slices of rye bread. She arranged tea on a silver platter, offering milk, honey and sugar cubes, insisting the traveler drink it all. *For the weary mind and tired body.*

When their eyelids were heavy from the poison, Lavinia would lead them to a back room and lay them to rest on a bed, carefully made with satin sheets and wool blankets. She'd place their heads on cotton pillows and take their shoes off. Then she lit candles by the bed and when they began to cry out because the hemlock was taking hold causing tremors and paralysis, she sang to them until they closed their eyes.

Then John would pull a lever to a trapdoor and the victim would cartwheel down into a spiked pit. Lavinia would smile and pour the tea out the window. Romantically gruesome. The husband-and-wife serial killers would then rummage through their pockets, bags and purses, collecting any valuables.

Eventually, the authorities caught on and arrested the murderous couple. John pleaded that he was a Christian and Lavinia smiled. They were both hung in the courtyard of the jail. Legend has it that while standing in front of the noose Lavinia yelled out to the crowd, "if you have a message you want to send to hell, give it to me and I'll carry it."

Lavinia and John were buried in a potter's field next to the jail. Weeds grow atop their rumored gravesite in a tangled mass of foliage. The whole time we toured the abandoned building my grandfather kept asking if I could feel Lavinia's presence or see her hauntingly beautiful smile and the vials of hemlock.

I didn't but I remember feeling weird the whole time I was in the jail. I felt like we were not supposed to have been there, it was not for the living. At the end of the tour, we stopped by Lavinia's cell. I spotted a graffiti smiley face in the bottom corner, J + L etched into the cement, enclosed in a heart. Could that have been from the star crossed, serial killing lovers John and Lavinia?

We left the car and walked through the front gate. I spotted Sheriff Walker standing in front of Grandpa's car with a furrowed brow while resting his hand unnaturally on his gun holster. He chewed on a toothpick and held a big gulp of Cherry Coke from the gas station. Classy.

"Has his car been here the whole time?" I asked with a hint of exasperation.

"Of course not," the sheriff shot back. "We've been by this place at least a dozen times since his disappearance. In fact, one of my deputies swung by here late yesterday afternoon and nothing was there. Your grandfather or someone must have parked the car here late last night."

Relax, I warned myself. Taking it out on the sheriff wasn't going to do any good. He seemed displeased as it was with sweat beaded along his receding hairline, dripping down his forehead, the sun glinted off his sheriff badge.

"Did you find anything else?" I asked in a much more docile tone.

"The forensic boys are on the way. Hopefully, they'll be able to find more but I did find something of interest."

The sheriff stopped then looked over my shoulder. "Charlie Parker, right?"

"Yes," Charlie answered.

"You saved me a trip. You have some explaining to do, son."

"What do you mean?" Charlie asked.

The sheriff leaned into the rolled down window of grandpa's car and pulled out a transparent plastic bag. He handed it to me. I opened it up and inside was a handwritten note that I recognized as Joe's writing. I read the brief note:

Alex, if you read this I have gone missing. Get in touch with Charlie Parker. He knows where to find me—Grandpa

Holy Toledo! Underneath my grandfather's plea was Poe's code from *The Gold Bug Island* story.

53‡‡†305))6;4826)4‡.)4‡);806*;48†8*
¶60))85;;]8;:‡*8†83(88)5*†;46(;88*96*
**?;8)*‡(;485);5*†2:*‡(;4956*2(5*—4)8*
¶8;4069285);)6†8)4‡‡;1(‡9;48081;8:8‡*
*1;48†85;4)485†528806*81(‡9;48;(88;4*
(‡?34;48)4‡;161;:188;‡?;

CHAPTER 3

NUMBERS STATIONS

The broiling hot afternoon caused sweat to bead along the sheriff's menacing brow. He swiped at his forehead and spit on the ground. I passed my grandfather's note to Charlie who read it before handing it back to the sheriff. Charlie seemed impassive as he shoved his hands into his pocket and pursed his lips.

"Why don't we step into the jail so I can have a few words with you in private," the sheriff said over to Charlie.

"You don't think I had anything to do with this, do you?" he answered a bit defensively.

"Son, you just read that note. It's obvious you're connected to this in some way. Let's go talk in private. This is not a request. We can do this here, or we can go down to the police station."

"Fine," Charlie answered.

"Why don't you just ask him whatever you need here?" I replied. "After all, this is about my grandfather."

The sheriff shot me a disapproving look, one riddled with rigid authority. He placed his palm onto the butt of his holster gun and readjusted his feet, staring at me like a crude, poorly chiseled limestone statue. "This is a police matter. You stay here. And another thing, do not go near your grandfather's car. The forensic boys are on their way down and I don't want you messing with or corrupting any potential evidence."

I started to protest because that was ridiculous considering he had just let both me and Charlie touch the bag and note. I only play a detective on TV but I'm sure our fingerprints contaminated that evidence. I decided to keep quiet.

The sheriff then turned to the deputy. "Don't let her near that car."

"Roger, boss," the deputy tipped his hat then winked at me. He pulled out a pouch of Big-League bubble gum and stuffed a huge wad into his mouth. He seemed like the kind of person who didn't bother spitting out his gum when it lost its flavor, but instead just added another piece. Then another and another.

I watched Charlie and the sheriff hoof it into the Old Jail to have their chat. Although it seemed more like an awkward shuffle. The sheriff waddling behind Charlie like some sort of preened puffin nudging him along.

I went over to my car, climbed up on the hood and sat there, contemplating. The only thing I knew for sure was that grandfather's note meant that he was alive, at least for now.

The whole situation was baffling. Why didn't grandpa just say where he was? Or with who? Grandpa was into collecting first edition mystery novels, and to be completely honest, I wasn't exactly surprised by these antics, just his aloofness.

I mean, he wasn't exactly the most communicative person, but he wasn't off-the-grid crazy either.

Questions continued to fill my mind: who had brought his car to the Old City Jail? Had his kidnappers not seen his note? Was it left there by mistake? More perplexing was the notion that whoever had abducted Grandpa knew his note was there and they wanted the police to find it. I was beginning to feel like a character from Criminal Minds.

But then an even more disturbing thought crossed my mind: Was it possible that Grandpa had driven the car there himself and then abandoned it for some reason? And how exactly was Charlie involved in all this and what was the deal with that Edgar Allen Poe code?

From my knowledge, Poe was just strange. Poverty was his muse, and he married his teenage cousin. I wrote a paper in school about his last days. Baltimore 1849, Poe, with his slicked back raven hair and pressed tweed coat, went missing for five days. Perhaps lost to the marsh, consumed by the mud he described in his poems. It was Election Day. Gunner's Hall, a polling location, and a man stumbles upon the delirious and scanty Poe. He's dressed in clothes much too large for him, as if someone just shoved him into a ratty button-down. Poe lays face-down in the gutter, suffering from a strange fever dream, and he calls out for someone named Reynolds and doesn't stop calling for Reynolds until he dies. Four days later. Alone.

I grabbed my head in between my hands massaging my throbbing temples. I wanted to scream. My brain was pounding, reverberating like a speaker belting out a heavy metal drum solo— Metallica playing for a crazed insomniac.

I ignored the pain and called my mom to give her the update about Grandpa. The phone rang a couple of times before she answered.

"Hey Mom," I said excitedly. "I'm down at the Old City Jail and they found Grandpa's car."

"I know," Mom interrupted.

"You know?"

"Well, of course dear. The sheriff called and told us all about it."

"Then why aren't you and Dad down here?"

"Honey, what can we do? Better to let the police manage the investigation and keep out of their way. We don't want to impede their investigation."

What in the heck was wrong with these people! My mom switched subjects and began droning on and on about the tennis tournament at the country club and the gluten free lasagna dish she concocted from eggplants and zucchini.

I set my cell on the hood of the car and stared up at the Old City Jail because I was on the verge of losing it. I took a deep breath as the Metallica drum solo picked up intensity.

At the corner of the building was an octagonal tower with a single small window. I stared up at it trying to fathom if my parents were actually my biological parents.

The sun was just above the roofline above the tower. A dark flash from inside the window caught my attention. I couldn't be certain, but it looked like a person, or a shadow had backed away from the window.

I shielded my eyes trying to block out the sun but whatever I thought I had seen was gone. I laughed nervously thinking maybe I had seen Lavinia Fisher's ghost. No, no, I am a normal girl. I am not Charlie Parker. I had to remind myself that I was not a deranged ghost-hunter who only eats Subway sandwiches, microwaveable dinosaur nuggets and pudding with sprinkles.

My grandfather would be convinced, however, that what I saw was, in fact, a ghost. God, I must be going insane. Apparitions of heat and dehydration and suddenly I'm on a

1 V show where they cleanse your house from spirits with sage and a clove of garlic and a convincing salt circle ritual.

I picked up my phone and my mom was still babbling on about something, vegan pizza and more country club affairs. "Mom," I interrupted. "Why isn't Dad down here?"

She stopped and answered nonchalantly, "Like I said, dear. We didn't want to interfere, and we knew you were going down there anyway."

"How'd you know I was here?" I asked with rising irritation.

"Because when the sheriff called, he told us he was going to call you and ask you to come down to the City Jail."

"Why would the sheriff have any reason for me to come down here?"

"I don't know. He mentioned something about bringing that Charlie Parker boy down with you because he had some questions to ask him."

Despite the hot humid day, a sudden chill ran through me. "Mom, how would the sheriff even know I was with Charlie?"

There was a long pause. "How would I know, sweetie."

"Okay whatever. I've got to go," I said in exasperation, clicking off my phone while my mom was in midsentence about the eggplant parmesan.

After about ten minutes the sheriff and Charlie came out of the jail. They ambled over like a parent and a child after a scolding. Charlie didn't look so happy. He walked past me over to passenger side door, blowing me off with a not-so-suave flick of the shoulder. "Let's go."

I looked back over to the sheriff. "How did you know I was with Charlie," I demanded.

"I don't know what you're talking about."

"My mother said you called her then you asked me to come down here because you knew I was with Charlie."

The sheriff gave me an alien-like stare and made that weird clicking noise in his throat again. "I have to get back to the station."

I watched him get into his police car, with those stupid mirrored sunglasses, and speed away kicking up a trail of dust, like some sort of a modern-day cowboy film scene. An old police cruiser instead of a horse, but same effect. I half-expected some twangy western music to play from a hidden speaker.

I got into my car and glared at Charlie who shrugged. "I'll explain later. Let's get out of here."

I pulled the car out of the City Jail and started driving back towards King Street, passing the smoothie shop and expensive antique stores. Neither of us said a word until out-of-the-blue my stomach made a loud gurgling noise.

Charlie laughed. "I'm hungry too. Let's get something to eat and we'll talk about it."

"No dinosaur nuggets, right?"

"Ha, ha," Charlie muttered under his breath.

"No Subway either."

"I understand!" he laughed.

"Where do you want to go," I asked.

"How 'bout The Blind Tiger. They have good burgers."

"Sounds good to me."

I parked on Broad Street, and we took a table in the outdoor courtyard. Though it was hot as Hades, the misting fans and shade made it feel ten degrees cooler.

"This place is pretty cool," I said to Charlie pointing at the old brick wall that surrounded the entire courtyard. "Can't believe I haven't been here before."

"It has an interesting history. I don't know if you saw it but inside there is a plaque with the building's history. "Blind Tiger" was a phrase that was used in South Carolina in the late 1800's and early 1990's to denote a place where you could go for illicit drinks or to gamble."

"Sounds like a place where you'd be right at home," I needled. "What did you and the sheriff talk about?"

"He asked me if I knew where Joe was."

"And do you?"

Charlie started to answer but waited as the waitress delivered our burgers. We both took bites then Charlie continued, "I might have got him involved or helped him get involved in something that he should have left alone."

"Exactly what is that supposed to mean?"

"It's hard explaining to someone like you."

"What do you mean someone 'like me'?"

"You live in the real world and . . ."

"C'mon," I cut him off. "Enough gibber jabber, just tell me what the heck you're talking about."

Charlie sighed. "Okay. Joe and I believe that there is, unseen by most, an underworld, a place that is just as real but not as brightly lit . . . a dark side."

"You're an idiot." I laughed.

Charlie started laughing too. "You like that, huh?"

"Yeah, that was actually pretty funny . . . reciting the opening monologue from that old TV show. What was it called?"

"Tales from the Dark Side."

"Yeah, right. I used to watch that show with my grandfather when I was a kid. I can't believe I still remembered it."

"I didn't think you'd recognize that. But even though those are not my words; it's kind of what we believe."

"Charlie, what do you really do?"

"I told you, I'm an investigator. I research unexplained mysteries and post my findings to my website."

"You have a website?"

"I don't advertise it but it's at www.Charlestonmystery.com. You should check it out? I do a podcast every month or so as well."

"Do you make any money?"

"No, not really," he laughed. "I get a little money from articles. A tiny bit of advertising comes in from my website. Occasionally, I actually get an investigative job. Mostly, it's some husband who wants me to convince their wife that they didn't see a ghost in the kid's bedroom. Or that the weird noises coming from the baby monitor doesn't mean that it's been hijacked by a demon. Stuff like that."

"Look Charlie, I don't care what you do or what crazy stuff you believe. I just want to find my grandfather. Can you help me?"

Charlie took a big swig of his iced tea and swallowed dramatically before continuing, "Of course I can help. But the first thing you need to know is that your grandfather and the sheriff have a very unusual relationship. You could say they are adversaries."

"Really," I exclaimed with a bit of shock. "I always thought they were kind of semi-friendly acquaintances?"

Although he annoyed me, the sheriff had the aura of a business acquaintance, a Friday night drinks at the bar kind of man. The kind of man who would offer to buy a communal plate of cheese fries, no split check.

"Yeah. I don't know about that," Charlie responded. "I think it may be more like keeping your friends close but your enemies even closer. He told me to be careful around him."

"Did he elaborate any more than that?"

"Sometimes your grandfather could get a little hard to understand. He talked metaphorically a lot. He believed that the sheriff was part of The Shadows. A dark, malevolent force seeking the world's or even the universe's dissolution."

"The Shadows as in some type of group or something?"

"He wouldn't elaborate more than that."

"Okay, that is really strange. We'll come back to that but what else did you and the sheriff talk about?"

"He just kept drilling me over and over about what I knew about that Numbers Station and the connection to Poe's code. But mostly, he kept asking me if Joe knew the location of the Numbers Station."

"That's weird. Why would he be so interested in where some creepy radio station is located?"

"I think the sheriff is more interested in finding the Numbers Station than finding your grandfather. Do you think there is any way you could get some more of Joe's files?"

"I don't really feel like upsetting my grandmother in light of everything but . . . " I looked at my watch and an idea popped into my head. "Grandma lives a very scheduled life. She should be leaving in half an hour to play bridge and have lunch—mimosas served with chicken salad sandwiches on wheat bread. Let's ride over there and see if she leaves. I know where they hide the spare key. I'll put these files back and grab some more. She'll never know."

With our fly-by-the-seat-of-our-pants plan in place we wolfed down the rest of our cheeseburgers then headed over to Grandma's house. I parked a few houses down in the opposite direction that Grandma would be leaving to go play bridge. Sort of stakeout-esque.

Much to our surprise, after five minutes of waiting the sheriff's cruiser came down the street and parked in her driveway.

Charlie and I looked at each, exchanging suspicious glances. Yep, it was confirmed. The sheriff, and quite possibly Grandma, were hiding something. I was 100% sure of that. He got out of the car and ambled up to the front door.

"What do you think that is about?" I asked.

Charlie shrugged and we watched as the sheriff walked in Grandma's house without even knocking.

"Okay, that's weird," I said. I didn't think that my grandma and the sheriff were on "no-knocking" terms. I mean, he wasn't exactly the kind of person she'd invite to after-church brunch served with sausage-egg quiche and lemonade from crystal glasses.

A few minutes later Grandma opened the door and they both stepped out. The sheriff opened his car door for her, and Grandma hopped in like it was no big deal and they drove off together. This definitely deviated from her bridge and lunch-mimosas penciled in on Tuesdays from 1:45-4:00.

"Stay here, I'll be back."

I jogged across the street and grabbed the spare key from underneath the flower box on the windowsill. I opened the door and called out instinctively, "Hello, anyone here?"

I felt like a cat thief while tip toeing down their foyer toward grandpa's office. I walked in and opened the drawer to the cabinet. I placed the files back in their spot and took five more of the Ford Files.

Easy enough, I thought as I turned to leave.

A crackling noise almost made me jump out of my skin. I turned and static erupted from the ham radio. I laughed nervously. I slowly walked over with the static eerily changing pitch and volume.

The static began to grow softer and then I thought I heard something. I bent down looking for the volume button and turned the dial to the loudest setting.

The static hissed and a barely audible voice emerged, "Dalton, Dalton. Are you there?"

The static began to grow louder muffling out the transmission. I had to turn the volume back down. The static noise softened, and the voice came back.

"Hello Dalton, do you copy? Dalton! Help me, I'm trapped."

A loud crack came from the radio and the voice and static abruptly ended. My heart was racing a mile a minute. I recognized the voice.

I picked up the microphone and clicked the button on the side. "Hello, hello. This is Alex. Can you hear me? Please tell me where you are?"

I desperately repeated the call a few more times but there was no answer. The radio had gone dead. No static. No voices. Nothing. Like everything had just evaporated like ripples atop a pond. I left the house and hurried across the street to the car.

"You got the files?" Charlie asked.

I held up the files in my hand.

"You okay? You look like you've seen a ghost."

"I didn't see one, but I heard one. I was in Grandpa's office and his ham radio started crackling and making static noises. Then I heard a voice calling for help saying he was trapped somewhere."

"That's weird?"

I looked at him. "No, the weird part was the person pleading for help was my grandfather."

CHAPTER 4

THE COWBOY

Grandpa Joe was alive! Of course, in that moment I didn't know what or how to feel or think. It was sort of a serious Twilight Zone conundrum. On one hand, I was ecstatic but, on the other (more ominous) hand, I knew he was in big trouble, whatever that meant.

And I had absolutely no semblance of a clue what I was supposed to do from here. Really, would you? I mean, for God's sake, this was a conspiracy theorist's dream come true and I, for one, fall into the "skeptic" category I was not exactly looking for ghosts or ghouls or parallel universes trapping Grandpa Joe in a time-warp where his only form of communication was a ham radio that had definitely seen better days.

I wanted to tell my parents but how would I explain that I broke into Grandma's house and heard grandpa's voice on the ham radio? They would first ground me, then have me committed to a psychiatric facility.

I could see myself being released years later after surviving on strawberry Jell-O cups while believing an alien invasion was imminent (which, at that point, I shouldn't have so easily disregarded).

43

We sat on Charlie's couch after our clandestine Ford Files theft trying to figure out who this Dalton person could be. The name was mundane, nothing that would stick in an off-hand conversation about the new owner of a bait shop or a car mechanic. The name didn't have a Jack the Ripper feel to it. Dalton might as well have been a clerical worker at a hedge fund company, working nine to five, wearing khakis on casual Fridays and drinking beers with the boys after work.

"Why do you think people like supernatural or paranormal movies or books?" Charlie asked out of the blue.

"I don't know, people just like to be entertained. They like to be scared, I guess. I mean, the last horror movie I saw in theaters was a waste of twelve dollars and a large soda and—"

Charlie shook his head. "For a pre-med student, you sure don't look too far below the surface, do you?"

"What is that supposed to mean?"

"You're right that entertainment and thrills are part of it but why do you really think people gravitate towards the supernatural or paranormal?"

"I don't know," I answered in exasperation.

"I think the underlying reason people like supernatural and horror books and movies so much is because if things like ghost or zombies are real, then that means there is life after death. So, death is not the end. There is something after our physical bodies die out."

"Very poetic, Mr. Charlie Parker," I replied. "But I'd rather suffer eternal darkness than transform into some lonely pathetic ghost trying to scare the bejeebers out of people for all of eternity. Or even worse condemned as a rotting corpse walking around in circles with my arms falling off. No thank you."

Charlie laughed. "Yeah, you have a point. All right let's get started. But first why don't I go pick us up a pizza."

"Sounds good, I'm starving."

Charlie left giving me an opportunity to check out his apartment a little more closely. It was a one-bedroom studio within a larger building that was at least a hundred years old. Charleston was one of the oldest cities in the country and for whatever reason that meant Charlestonians liked old stuff including where they lived. Antiques were the rage; an aged desk was equivalent to fine cheese.

But despite the obvious age of the building there was a certain charm to it with its vaulted ceilings, faded brick walls and distressed hardwood floors.

A typical theme in Southern gothic architecture, like someone was trying to rebuild the French quarter within a background of palmetto trees and marsh. Which, in all honesty, had already happened in the city with the French Quarter recognized as a national landmark: wharves and cobblestone streets, winding along the waterfront. Quaintly painted buildings, climbing ivy, street names like Prioleau, Poulnot, and Perrier (kidding about the Perrier, but I wouldn't put it past Charlestonians).

But Charlie's furniture, that's another story. Everything looked handpicked from someone's trash pile. His choice of décor definitely was not southern charm or fine vintage ware that people went out of their way to scout out in thrift stores and estate sales.

The kitchen had a discolored, long butcher block that served as a table with one bar stool. On the far wall of the kitchen there was a large window with a view overlooking King Street. If you looked past the cars and middle-aged women, it's as if you can imagine what the city looked like hundreds of years ago. Brick streets and old building facades.

The living area had a single couch and a black leather chair with a faded bean bag in the corner (which seemed to accurately reflect his career path). Interestingly, I didn't see a TV anywhere. In today's world who lives without a TV? Old sci-fi and pulp horror posters were hanging haphazardly across the walls.

In between the living area and the bedroom was Charlie's workspace. A large desk wedged in the corner reminded me of Grandpa's office at home. Stacks of books, files and papers rose from floor to ceiling. How did he ever get any work done in this mess?

There was no TV. No family photos. I started to feel a bit weird as though I was prying in his personal life peeling back the layers of his pathetic existence in the apartment, which in retrospect, was exactly what I was doing.

I went back to the couch and sat down trying to stifle a yawn. Opening the new Ford File, I found it hard to concentrate because I kept hearing over and over again the eerie woman's voice repeating Poe's code followed by the strange musical notes and then Grandpa's voice calling for help. I put the file down and yawned again. I stretched out on the couch. *I'll rest for just a few minutes* I thought as my eyelids suddenly got very heavy.

I didn't know where I was or how I got there but it was dark and cold, and the air smelled wrong. Dank like an attic, musty. Whatever this place was, I knew I was not supposed to be here. The sort of feeling you get when you are at a gas station late at night, pumping gas and looking over your shoulder.

Then it dawned on me I was searching for Grandpa. He was here. It was like a psychic intuition. I looked around the room lit only by lanterns attached to the stone wall.

Suddenly, moonlight filtered down from the cathedral window and a knowledge filled me. This is The Light. The source of all life in the universe. The virtuous, heroic forces preserving order and goodness. Their deeds and the powers they wield make up the stuff of legends... if not myths. But wherever there is The Light, there is The Shadow. The dark, malevolent forces seeking the universe's dissolution.

A ham radio was on a small bench transmitting an eerie woman's voice who was repeating the incessant series of numbers from Poe's code.

Her shrill voice was driving me crazy. It felt like my whole body was about to shatter into a million pieces, scattered around the room like shards of glass. I ran over to the radio and turned the volume control down, but nothing happened. The woman methodically just kept repeating the same numbers over and over again in her tormented voice.

I picked up the ham Radio and threw it against the wall. I stared down at the broken radio. Tubes and wires splattered everywhere, like disemboweled intestines. The voice stopped but my peace was short lived because the numbers started transmitting again. *How could the radio still be transmitting?* I thought in disbelief, staring at its wiry guts on the floor.

My flight sense took over and I saw a small door behind me. I turned the handle releasing a waft of dreadful smelling air that hit me like a ton of bricks.

A narrow dark tunnel led from the room. I stumbled through the darkness in a claustrophobic panic. The tunnel emptied into a cavernous room causing me to stop dead in my tracks. I wasn't alone. The sheriff stood in the middle of the room.

He looked at me and said, "The worst mistake that you can make is to think you're alive when really you're asleep in life's waiting room. Welcome to the Void, Alan. What will you choose? The Light or The Shadow?"

I jumped up from the couch in a cold sweat.

"Jeez," Charlie replied. "You okay? You must have been having one heck of a nightmare."

My heart was beating a mile a minute and I felt dizzy.

"You all right?" he repeated.

"Yeah," I managed to reply. "Could you get me a glass of water?"

"Sure thing."

I sat back down on the couch trying to catch my breath. Charlie brought me the water and I drank it down in three gulps, helping to slow my racing heart.

"What time is it?" I asked, noticing it had turned dark outside.

"Nine-thirty," he answered. "I came back with the pizza, but you were zonked out. So, I just let you sleep."

"I was having a nightmare."

"Yeah, I guessed that. You know, a lot of people believe that dreams are really just your consciousness slipping into an alternative reality or a quantum parallel universe."

"Jeez, don't you ever give it a rest. Please shut up and give me a slice of pizza."

"Certainly."

He handed me the pizza box. There was one-and-a-third slices left. I gave him an evil look and he shrugged his shoulders with a sheepish grin. "I was hungry, and I didn't want to wake you. So, what did the next Ford File reveal?"

"Well, I didn't get very far before I zonked out, but I got far enough to think old Grandpa might have been going a little crazy in his older years."

"Why do you say that?"

"I'll let you read the file. He believed he had contacted an alternative reality or parallel universe through his ham radio. And this is where it gets even crazier." I paused to take another bite of pizza then continued, "He thought he had made contact with Edgar Allen Poe."

"I guess that is the reason why he was obsessed with that code."

"Yeah, but it gets even weirder. He was convinced that the code that led to Captain Kidd's treasure was a smokescreen, or really a metaphor. He believed that the code led to something else bigger than treasure."

"Okay, where did he think the code led to?"

"A parallel universe. Or multiverse as he referred to it." A loud knock interrupted me. "Expecting someone?"

Charlie shook his head and walked over to the door. He slowly opened it and stepped back as the most dangerous-looking man I had seen stepped inside Charlie's apartment.

He looked exactly like an evil cowboy out of a spaghetti western-slash-horror flick. He stood at least six-foot-four with a thick beard. He wore a black cowboy hat with long hair that fell past his shoulders. Despite the fact that it was summer he wore a black trench coat and thick pants made from burlap.

Even his pupils were black as coal. He looked like a deranged cowboy who had risen straight from the depths of hell. If this was one of Charlie Parker's associates, I should use his arrival as a cue to leave.

"Can I help you?" Charlie asked a bit nervously.

The Cowboy from hell looked over at me. "My name is Dalton Rand. I know where your grandfather is."

CHAPTER 5

EUREKA

Dalton! Could this be the same person I heard Grandpa calling for on the ham radio? Nothing is a coincidence. I mean, come on, creepy cowboy, creepy radio, creepy ghosts, creepy files, creepy creepers. He was the embodiment of creepy and thus led me to the only conclusion I could draw from his presence: we were definitely in trouble.

"Where is my grandfather?" I blurted out wishing I had kept my tone a little more hospitable.

"Actually, ma'am I misspoke. I know where he isn't. And where he isn't is the more important answer to your question."

Men. What is it with these cryptic answers? Yes or no should suffice. All incapable of answering the most basic questions, seeming to find pleasure in answering the simplest question with another question or a riddle. Dalton smiled revealing a set of decaying teeth. He stared at us with fleeting, black eyes. All I could think of was man, he needed a trip to the dentist.

"Okay, where is he not?" I asked, figuring I had to play his game.

"He's not here." Dalton answered in a clipped, almost sounding, but not quite, Texas accent.

"No shoot Sherlock," Charlie responded.

The cowboy slowly turned to Charlie with a menacing stare that sent a shiver down my spine. I made a note not to bad mouth the creepy cowboy in any form or fashion.

His black eyes seem to bore through Charlie, and I grimaced thinking about what would happen next. He started to reach inside his trench coat. My brain urged me to scream "run for it" but instead of pulling out a six shooter he withdrew a rolled up, faded yellow manuscript.

He handed me the manuscript. "This is where your grandpa is, ma'am."

I held the parched papers in my hands like it was a swarming mass of poisonous spiders and venomous snakes. Dangerous and on the verge of delivering a death sentence. It could've been laced with arsenic or hemlock or whatever poison this Dalton most likely dabbled in. The paper was old and so brittle I was worried it would disintegrate in my hands.

Eureka by Edgar Allen Poe, spelled out in delicate ink letters, curling on the paper.

I looked back up at the cowboy. "I don't understand."

The cowboy stared over at Charlie and asked, "You have any whiskey, son?"

"Ah, no but I have beer?"

"That will do. This may take a while for you to read but it will explain where he is, then we'll have some work to do."

Charlie gave Dalton a bottle of beer which he proceeded to open with his teeth, spitting the bottle top across the room like a true movie villain.

He chugged almost half the beer in one gulp. He propped his boots up, cracked and dirty, and wiped droplets of beer from his chin. He appeared nearly as cracked and dirty as his shoes and something about the way he moved made him appear pixelated as if he had been peeled from an old cinema film.

Charlie looked at me in dismay and I sat down on the couch and began reading. *Eureka* was a long story for Poe, almost 150 pages, and even though I consider myself a speed reader it took both of us a couple of hours to finish. During that entire time, the cowboy sat in the kitchen chair staring off into space with those vacant, black eyes, shining like crow plumage, while drinking beer after beer, never uttering a single word. How strange you must be thinking. Yes, very. But you could bet that I definitely was not going to question any of it.

After we finished Poe's *Eureka* the "Cowboy from Hell" proceeded to give us a 30-minute tutorial on the substance of the story including a wide range of non-cowboy subjects including physics, something called Olber's Paradox, cosmology and multiverses.

Eureka was quite unlike any of Poe's normal macabre stories and poems that I had read in high school. Far different from the horror of stories like *The Raven or The Tell-Tale Heart*. This was more of a scholarly essay on the origins of the universe. And even more shocking, Dalton was an expert in the matter and patiently explained to us that Poe knew in 1848 what it took physicists another 100 years to theorize. The eloquence of his words ebbing and flowing like Charleston marshes, an ecosystem complex and vibrant and microscopic, it would take years of analysis to understand.

Back in Poe's day the consensus was that the universe was static and eternal. His essay suggested that the universe had exploded into being from a single "primordial particle" in "one instantaneous flash" or what we now refer to as the Big Bang Theory. A glorious moment of nothing into everything.

He also theorized that the universe is finite in time and space and that the velocity of light was measurable and fixed. I had no idea how Poe knew all this back then. Wasn't he supposed to be a horror writer who consumed way too much absinthe?

Amazingly, Poe also deduced because of these scientific constants that it was not only possible but probable that there were other universes in other dimensions with different laws of nature. All obscured by the linearity of human thought.

The most profound aspect of *Eureka* was Poe's certainty that the soul continues to survive after death, hence, his fascination with ghouls, death and the afterlife. The intangible filaments of the human soul, the monsters that lurk just beneath our line of sight and the grasp of the dead seem to have over us. Staring into the ghoulish face of the creepy cowboy, I began to believe Poe wrote with some sort of accuracy.

The cowboy finished and I wearily looked out the kitchen window. The sun was threatening to peak over the horizon, eerily red like the rind of a blood orange.

My mind was spinning from the information and the lack of sleep and the Charleston heat and Dalton's stare and the stench of beer and what he was suggesting. Insanity. At least that was what the logical part of my, I am supposed to be going to college to study pre-med, brain was suggesting. Logistics downed in IPA.

My gut was telling me something different my brain didn't appreciate. Like I've said, I'm a skeptic. A pupil of Plato's Academy one could say.

This brought me back to what Charlie had said earlier and it began to make sense. To write such horrific and supernatural things, Poe had to believe in them. Genuinely believe in them.

I stood up keeping one eye on the cowboy, afraid that he was going to whip a gun from his trench coat and challenge me to a duel in the alley adjacent to the Subway. A fly lazily landed on his forehead, and he swatted at it vigorously. The heat was stifling and tiresome and I yawned as I walked over to the kitchen window.

The sky had transitioned from blackness to a faint orange-yellow color signaling a new day, one that held a little less optimism than the day before. I turned and looked back at the cowboy who, despite drinking every single one of Sam's beers, looked neither inebriated nor tired.

"What do we do now?" I asked him.

"We'll go fetch your grandfather and bring him back here." He reached into his trench coat again and pulled out a single sheet of faded yellow paper. He handed me the paper with Poe's code from *Gold Bug Island*. Next to the code was the translation. I read it aloud so Charlie could hear.

"A good glass in the bishop's hostel in the devil's seat
twenty-one degrees and thirteen minutes northeast and
by north main branch seventh limb east side
shoot from the left eye of the death's-head
a bee line from the tree through the shot fifty feet out."

"That is the recognized translation from Poe's code from the *Gold Bug Island* but there is another one, the real one."

"And what is that?" I asked.

"Meet me at Fort Moultrie tonight at three."

"That is not an answer. Where is my grandfather and

what do you have to do with this?"

"You'll find out tonight."

Irritation aside, there was nothing Charlie or I could do? He'd crush us like two palmetto bugs which was a gentile Charleston name for a cockroach.

"Okay, three a.m. at Fort Moultrie," I replied. "Let me ask you a strange question Dalton. As Poe lay dying he called out for a man named Reynolds. You said your last name is Reynolds."

"Yes, it is." He stood, adjusted his cowboy hat and walked out the front door.

Funny how the mind words. Of all the things I should have been considering in regard to this terrifying encounter, my brain fixated on one absurd thought. How did Dalton get to Charlie's? Did he take an uber? A rent-a-car? Or does he have a horse tied up outside?

CHAPTER 6

FORT MOULTRIE

I went home, crawled into bed, and slept away most of the day, my tormented dreams repeating themselves like a scratch on an old record. The ghoulish figure from the jail window receding into the shadows over and over again with terrified voices calling to me over radio broadcasts and demented cowboys chasing me across burned-out prairies.

By the time I woke up, it was getting dark, the sun thinning out across the horizon like egg yolk. The sight would have been pretty, if I didn't have the knowledge that Grandpa Joe was floating around in some ghost dimension or that a demonic cowboy was expecting us at a haunted fort that may serve as a bridge to another dimension.

I waited a few more hours before sneaking out of the house and heading over to Charlie's. I parked outside his apartment and texted him.

Even late into the night a mix of college students, locals and tourists streamed down the sidewalks heading back to their hotels, homes or God knows where. No doubt some were searching for that elusive last call bar to continue the night a little longer. The street smelled of a crosswind of the ocean and old books and I grew suddenly nostalgic for the landscape.

The night was incredibly hot and sweaty. The Southern hospitality bordered on insanity, nights like this made you long for the marsh. Until of course, you realize once again that a deranged, ill-tempered cowboy is expecting you. Then everything is a little less nostalgic.

Still, here I was. It was like a painting outside, a modicum of colors: copper pot, sea salt, tangerine, pink Chablis. The sound of locals twisting knives into half-moon oysters and sucking out the bivalves from their shells. The moon sat like a pearl on the Atlantic and a woman lit a cigarette behind an old brick building, smoke harpooning through the air.

A sudden thought overcame me. I was supposed to be starting college in six weeks. What was I doing? Sneaking out in the middle of the night with a paranormal investigator to meet some strange, deranged cowboy so we could break into a national monument to find my grandfather who might or might not have slipped into a parallel universe.

Yep, it's official, I have completely lost my mind.

That thought drifted away when I caught a glimpse of something in the alley across the street. A figure was lurking just inside the alley. What the heck! I squinted my eyes trying to get a better look. I couldn't tell what I was looking at with the passing cars, streams of people and the sea mist converging with the dim streetlights.

I swear though, whatever it was it didn't look real, the figure looked like a shadow. Then I remembered my weird dream about the sheriff and choosing between something called The Light and The Shadow.

The outline of the person wavered. They faded in and out, the way a candle flickers in a windowsill from a distance. I started to open the door to get a better look when Charlie jumped in the car scaring the bejeebers out of me.

"Damn it," I half-yelled acknowledging that the "possible" existence of ghosts had turned me into a crazy woman!

"You okay?" he asked.

I turned toward him. "Take a look across the street."

"Yeah, what about it?"

I looked back toward the alley. Whatever I thought I saw was gone, or maybe I had slipped across the abyss of insanity. Do people who are going insane know they are?

"Ah, nothing," I finally answered. "I just thought...never mind. Let's go meet Dalton."

Charlie gave me an odd look, but didn't question it and said, "Sounds good."

We drove over the near empty Cooper River Bridge in silence. I couldn't shake the image of that weird person lurking in the alley. Their milky silhouette burned into the dank alley light. I wanted to tell Charlie, but I also didn't want to sound paranoid bordering on delusional.

I decided to keep quiet, chalking it up to an over-imaginative mind, tricks of light combined with my tiredness and the imminent stress of retrieving my grandfather from a parallel dimension.

"When was the last time you've been to Fort Moultrie?" Charlie asked.

"Not since middle school. You know, the standard annual school field trip."

"Yeah."

"How about you?" I asked.

Charlie didn't answer.

"Something wrong?"

"I was at Fort Moultrie a few months ago," he finally answered apologetically.

"Okay, so what? You like old forts. Nothing to be ashamed of. I mean, for God's sake, your business card job description reads Paranormal Investigator. Heck, you've probably starred in an episode of Ghost Hunter."

"We broke into the fort late at night," he interrupted.

"Who's we?"

Charlie hesitated then answered, "Your grandfather and me."

I almost slammed down the brake pedal which would not have been a good idea since we were in the middle of the bridge.

"And you are telling me this now?"

"Look, I just met you a couple of days ago. Give me a break, I'm telling you now."

He had a point, so I took a deep breath and asked politely, "And why did you and my grandfather break into Fort Moultrie?"

"Your grandfather thought he had discovered where the Numbers Station was broadcasting from."

"And let me guess, he thought it was from inside Fort Moultrie?"

"That is what your grandfather believed."

"Lucky me. How'd he come up with that theory?"

"He told me that one of his ham radio buddies was some kind of communications expert and he was able to triangulate the broadcast to the fort."

"But why did he ask you to go with him? I didn't realize y'all were such buddies."

"Alex, like I told you, we're in the same business. It's a small club. I understood why he wanted me to go, and I didn't ask any questions."

Charlie's response seemed more than lame considering an old man was asking for help to break into a national monument.

"And what did you find?"

"Nothing. Well, not exactly. We didn't discover some lady in a room broadcasting Poe's Code if that is what you are asking."

"Okay . . . go on."

"It's hard to explain."

"Jeez, Charlie just tell me what happened."

"We arrived a little after three in the morning and scaled the wall. You know, sort of MacGyver style. The moon was full, so we had plenty of light along with our flashlights. We searched the outside grounds first not expecting to find anything but just to cover the bases. You remember when I told you that the Numbers Station Poe broadcast started every 33rd day at 3:30?"

"Yes."

"That is the reason we were there, on that day, at that time. It had been 33 days since the last broadcast, so we waited until 3:30 a.m. And at 3:30 Joe got a call from one of his ham buddies who told him the broadcast had started. Your grandfather had a lock cutter, and we started searching different sections of the fort trying to find where the broadcast was coming from. The fort's subdivided into sections from different time periods. We started in the front and moved backwards toward the ocean. We couldn't figure out how the transmission could have originated from inside the fort because we couldn't locate it. We began searching the oldest part of the fort built during the American Revolution. There we started to hear the broadcast. It sounded like it was radiating from inside the fort walls, but we couldn't pinpoint an exact location. But that's when we found the side tunnel or passageway."

Charlie stopped talking. I turned toward him. He had blank look on his face. "What's wrong?"

"Here's what's really strange," he answered. "We both knew the layout of Fort Moultrie like the backs of our hands."

"So?"

"So that tunnel that we came across doesn't exist."

"What do you mean it doesn't exist? Are you suggesting that it just spontaneously appeared somehow? You could have gotten lost or maybe you were in the wrong area?"

"We weren't. I went back to the fort the next day during regular hours thinking I had lost my mind, but the tunnel was not there."

"That doesn't make any sense."

"Does any of this make any sense?

"Good point."

"Anyway," Charlie continued, "at that point I wasn't turning back so I followed your grandfather down the passageway. It was twisting and dark but there were gas lanterns every fifty feet or so and we had flashlights. Besides the fact that the tunnel shouldn't exist, the most alarming aspect was that the tunnel was leading downward which was impossible because of the water table in that area. There is a reason why Charleston doesn't have basements. The whole area is practically under water.

"Anyway, we followed the tunnel for about five minutes until eventually we came to a dead end. There was a door and from inside we could hear the lady broadcasting the Numbers Station. I don't know what it was, but the broadcast felt like someone was driving a hot poker in my brain, twisting it around. It was maddening."

"Your grandfather tried to open the door, but it was locked. He had brought a backpack and inside he had a lock kit and I…"

"Wait, you're saying my grandfather had a lock kit in a backpack on your secret MacGyver mission?" I interrupted.

"Yeah, don't you keep a lock kit on you? It's like a first aid kit for people in our business, you never know when you'll need one."

"Right, thanks for the advice. Continue on."

Charlie cleared his throat, "I remember asking him if we really wanted to find out what was on the other side of the door? Of course, he dismissed me and after a few minutes he was able to pick the lock."

"Jeez, Charlie, I'm going to have to pull the car over. What was behind the door?"

"Nothing."

"What do you mean there was nothing? I thought you heard the lady?"

"We did but when we opened the door there was no one inside. It was a small, dimly lit semi-circle stone room with a low rock ceiling. There was no furniture except on the far wall was a small desk covered in a thick layer of dust. The center of the desk was dust free about the exact size of what could have been a ham radio. Stuck to the wall was this."

Charlie handed me the paper. I took a quick glance at it and gasped. It was one of those old-fashioned WANTED DEAD OR ALIVE posters. You know the ones in the Clint Eastwood westerns where he's a bounty hunter hired to go track down some murderous fugitive for the reward money.

But this reward poster was old and faded and looked real.

I stared at the poster with my mouth agape. WANTED DEAD OR ALIVE FOR MURDER REWARD $200. Underneath the bold caption was a black and white image of Dalton Reynolds aka the deranged cowboy dated April 1829.

"Is this some kind of joke?"

"That's what we found."

"Ok, I'm not even going to be able to articulate everything wrong with this but one: you realize that this is the guy we are about to meet. And two: he's a MURDERER!"

"Suspected," Charlie interrupted.

"And three: the wanted poster dated 1829. It can't be real."

"Looks real to me but I haven't got it carbon dated yet."

"Oh, of course, you haven't gotten it carbon dated! So, let me get this straight. We are going to meet some deranged cowboy who we know nothing about so we can break into a national monument. Oh, and by the way, the cowboy's wanted for a murder committed in 1829. And he believes my grandfather is in a parallel universe with Edgar Allen Poe. You don't see anything wrong with this asinine plan?"

Charlie didn't bother to answer so I continued, "I should've gotten a will notarized or something, because there is no way I'm going to survive tonight."

Charlie shrugged. "You have assets?"

"What! No, I don't have any assets. I have $36 in my checking account. I'm eighteen."

"Well, then technically you really don't need a will except maybe if you wanted to let your family know what they should do with your body."

"Shut up," I snapped.

"Okay. But you want to get your grandfather back, right?"

"I'm not so sure anymore," I answered sarcastically. "I mean, of course I do. But I also don't want to die or end up in jail or heaven forbid, stuck in another dimension. Let me ask you something Charlie. What exactly is your motivation in this?"

"Answers."

Then it finally hit me. Duh, how could I be so dense?

"Tonight, is the 33rd night since the last broadcast isn't it?"

"Correct."

We rode a few minutes in silence and every rational brain cell was telling me to stop the car, turn around and go home. But the irrational and stupid brain cells won out. I was pot committed—All In—as they say in Texas Hold 'Em. I didn't really want to think too hard about my odds.

We drove the rest of the way to Fort Moultrie with the radio playing some lame pop song that neither one of us recognized but neither one of us bothered to change. I parked the car in a residential part near the fort, so we didn't attract unwanted attention and we walked about a quarter mile to the fort in darkness.

The cicadas hummed and you could hear the ocean off in the distance, churning ominously. We were supposed to meet Dalton on the backside of the fort closest to the ocean. At this point I really was beginning to wish I had penned that will.

As we came around the back wall of the fort, I made Charlie go first and we spotted Mr. Dalton Reynolds aka Wanted Dead or Alive for murder committed in 1829. He had a makeshift rope ladder thrown over the wall.

"Hey," I called out as we cautiously approached.

He just grunted.

"Listen Dalton, there are a few things we'd like to ask you before we go into the fort," Charlie replied.

"What?" he replied in a non-too-friendly tone.

Charlie handed him the WANTED poster. Dalton stared down at it. "I don't read."

"It says you are wanted for murder," I replied.

"So."

"So," I almost yelled. Control your temper, Alex, I had to remind myself. For God's sake this guy could take me out with a single punch like I was a wet Kleenex. I looked over at Charlie who appeared more nervous than I had ever seen him in the brief period of time I'd known him.

"I don't think this is a good idea," I replied to Charlie. "Let's get out of here."

I turned to leave when I heard a loud click. "Hold it."

I stopped dead in my tracks and turned around. Dalton was pointing a pistol directly at me. At that point, I shouldn't have been surprised, but my stomach dropped as I stared down the dark barrel. I mean with the knowledge that he was a murderer (suspected, Charlie's voice rang through my head), I realized I should've stayed in the car. Stranger danger, you know.

"I am here to take you to your grandfather," Dalton stressed the work "take".

"Why? What do you care?"

"You'll just have to find out for yourself. But you want your grandfather back, right?"

My mouth opened but I couldn't form any words and just nodded.

Charlie stepped up to Dalton brazenly considering there was a loaded gun aimed at his face. "Tell us what's going on or we're not going in there with you. You can shoot me right now but that is the deal."

Dalton spit out a wad of chewing tobacco. "I don't think you're in a position to demand anything. I could just shoot both of you and be done with it."

I looked at Charlie and then back at Dalton and we didn't dare move.

Dalton lowered his gun. "Your grandfather found a portal when he deciphered Poe's Code. The Numbers Station allowed him to travel to our world but in doing so he has upset the balance of our existence. He does not belong there. I came to get you to bring him back."

"Why couldn't you just send him back here?" Charlie asked. "Why do you need us?"

"There are forces at work that I don't have any control over. It's complicated but you'll understand better once were there."

"I think we are going to need more than that to take a leap of faith and trust you." Charlie responded.

Dalton sighed as if annoyed by our measly mortal presence. "Worlds, universes are like tiny bubbles in an infinite ocean. They spring into existence then obliterate themselves all the time. But the one constant that these bubble universes or multiverses have is that they are made of energy, just like us. And energy cannot be destroyed, it can only change forms.

The place where I come from is far different from the place you inhabit. It resembles this world, but it isn't. Natural laws that apply here, don't necessarily apply there and vice versa. For whatever reason Poe is fond of your grandfather, at least for now. He is from a modern world, a world that most of us have no desire to introduce into ours. His closeness to Poe is a detriment to our world and we can't let that continue."

"Why?" I asked.

"Our world came into existence from Poe's energy."

"Are you saying Poe created your world? Like some kind of a God?" Charlie asked incredulously.

"All universes are created from a single energy force. And if that energy force is what you want to call God, then yes, Poe is our creator. But our world is relatively new, and it is still being created."

Charlie looked at me. "You don't have to do this. I can go alone."

"We are wasting time. The broadcast is about to start," Dalton replied.

I thought for a second. Maybe Dalton was right, and I needed to trust him. After all, Grandpa was calling for Dalton to help him. I had a bad feeling if I didn't do this, Grandpa was gone for good. This was my one and only opportunity.

"I'm going," I said and started climbing the rope ladder over the fort's walls.

I scaled the wall and waited for Charlie and then Dalton. We walked across the grounds toward the sound of crashing waves from the ocean. Dalton opened a gate that led to a covered section of the fort.

Charlie whispered, "This is the part of the fort that led us to the Numbers Station room."

We followed Dalton down the tunnel and around a bend. After a few minutes he stopped dead in his tracks and turned to his left. Cut out of the stone wall was a wooden door.

"That's it," Charlie said just as I began hearing an eerie voice repeating numbers over and over again. It was a shrill woman's voice, numbing and cold. It was the same voice as the one from my dream. The voice could only be described like old carnival music or a theremin or a sound bite from a lonely blue whale crying at the bottom of the sea. Either way, haunting. My brain started to revolt at the sound.

Dalton slowly opened the door causing my heart to skip a beat because I didn't know what we would find but there was no woman. Dalton stepped inside the dimly lit stone room.

On a ledge on the far side of the room was a ham radio. It began to crackle and static blared from the speaker. Though it was a relief not to see an old lady huddled in the corner of the room, the ham radio was more ominous, tarnished, but still shining like someone had tried to clean it recently.

We stepped inside and I asked Dalton, "Where are we going?"

"Dark Charleston," he grunted.

Before I had a chance to react, to back out, to say adios creepy cowboy, the door slammed shut engulfing us in darkness. The wailing of the ham radio grew dim, farther away, then darkness and complete silence.

CHAPTER 7

DARK CHARLESTON

In a flash the darkness that had engulfed us at Fort Moultrie was gone. Well, sort of. We were no longer at Fort Moultrie but standing in the middle of a strange-looking version of Battery Park in downtown Charleston. The laws of physics could not even begin to explain how we ended up here. This was definitely not a Mass X acceleration problem on a worksheet, and I did not even try to fathom it: simply put, I didn't want a headache.

The Battery is located on the lower shore of the Charleston Peninsula bordered by both the Ashley and Cooper Rivers which empty into the Charleston Harbor and then into the Atlantic Ocean. The little park is lined with statues, fountains and expensive waterfront houses making it a prime tourist and picnicking location. A delightful place for a morning jog and usually, the harbor's briny waves gently lapped against the concrete walls with boats bobbing along the surface.

But not here. Oh no, you would definitely not want to lay out your towel, scones, and blackberry preserves for a nice afternoon picnic in the shade of a large oak. I looked around and instinctively knew this was a different version of the Charleston I grew up in. Dalton was right, this was Dark Charleston.

The air felt dark, musty, polluted in a weird way like dirty light filtering through slats in an attic creating long disturbing shadows. I stared around trying to grasp the enormity of what had just happened. A terrifying thought crossed my mind, one I should have thought through a little more carefully.

What if this is all a trap and I am stuck in Dark Charleston forever?

I involuntarily jumped as an eerie sounding siren erupted from behind us. I turned toward the far side of the Battery and spotted a huge bell tower where the sound was emanating from.

"That bell tower doesn't exist in Charleston," I replied.

"Uh, huh." Charlie mumbled.

Poor guy was in shock and to be completely honest, I wasn't sure if it was from dread or excitement. Like he could've been a kid entering a candy store (albeit a candy store filled with ghosts and monsters not chocolate bars), or he could've been a kid who stayed up past his bedtime watching a horror movie in the basement then was tasked with the arduous journey up two flights of dark stairs to his bedroom.

The clock on the enormous tower read 3:33. Which was about the time we had entered the room at Fort Moultrie but something about the time didn't seem right. It felt more like twilight during a really cloudy day. Also, I could make out an orb which must have been the sun just above the horizon, but it was in the wrong place.

"Why is the sun rising in the west?" I asked to no one in particular.

"It's not rising," Dalton said, spitting some tobacco juice next to my shoe. "It's setting. It is afternoon here."

Then I noticed he was right: the sun was falling in the west, not rising in the east. I glanced at Charlie and said, "We've somehow lost or gained twelve hours?"

He shrugged his shoulders and for once looked as terrified as I felt in this abysmal landscape.

I turned completely around to get a better look at The Battery. In my Charleston, beautiful oak trees covered in swaths of Spanish moss lined the park. Horse drawn carriages filled with tourists would gaze in awe at the magnificent antebellum houses, all white columned and pristine as pastel pastries in a coffee shop. A gazebo standing in the center of the park for weddings with statues of famous Charlestonians and armory from wars past. The grounds were always immaculate and litter free.

But not here.

Here, The Battery looked like a combination of an old-world cemetery and a toxic wasteland in a post-apocalyptic movie. Old stone grave markers were haphazardly strewn across the park. Some had crumbled while others had toppled over. A few trees stood in various states of decay and women trudged through the dirt in long, aged dresses, shredded at the bottoms. They carried dainty lace umbrellas resembling those sold at the market today. But theirs were torn and tattered filled with holes. Just like the earth, pockmarked with little divots and shrapnel.

The brick facades of the antebellum houses were uneven, patched with red clay and pebbles dug up from the ground. A big chestnut mare dragged a small wooden cart filled with rotting fruit, potato sacks, and cannon balls. The man riding the horse hurried it along with a whip on the rear, bruised peaches spilling out of the cart.

It was like everything here was slowly disintegrating.

The grass was spotty, unkempt and greyish. Where there used to be sidewalks and a paved road for carriage rides and cars, there was just a dirt road. In the center of The Battery should have stood a beautiful gazebo but instead gallows laid claim and to my abject horror a half-dozen bodies hung from the limbs of a giant rotting oak tree next to the bell tower.

"I wonder what those guys did?" Charlie asked.

Dalton just grunted and mumbled something under his breath. He fit the landscape perfectly. Charlie, on the other hand, looked absolutely ridiculous in his The Monkees band tee shirt and jeans and, if the world didn't seem to be on the precipice of completely falling apart, I could've laughed.

I forced myself to look away and stared across Charleston Harbor over to where Patriot's Point in Mount Pleasant would usually be. From this location normally you would see the World War Two aircraft carrier, The Yorktown, and past that out in the harbor the island where Fort Sumter had stood for centuries.

Fort Sumter had the unique distinction of being the starting points for both the Revolutionary and Civil Wars. But now, there was no fort. Instead, a monstrous medieval castle stood in its place, pillared and constructed from old stone.

Large purple flags fluttered from the sides as if some reminder of a glorious conquest. It was almost regal, if not for the fact that the flags were in tatters. This place was the evil cousin of Charleston, far different from the quaint, cobblestoned city printed in glossy travel magazines advertising its history, Southern charm, and multitude of five-star restaurants. On top of all that our tour guide was a murderous cowboy who had shoved a pistol into our faces and dragged us here in the first place.

The rough harbor wake expanded the way a moat might, as though adapting to a threat. The tinted water, the color of algae, was like the film at the top of an unkempt aquarium.

The aircraft carrier was also gone, replaced with four ships that looked straight out of a Pirates of the Caribbean movie. I half expected Jack Sparrow to swing around and whisk us away on a more light-hearted Disney franchise adventure. Unfortunately, that was not the case.

"Let's go," Dalton replied, the wooden heels of his leather boots clacking ominously against the red stone.

We followed the cowboy in the direction of what used to be the historic district of Charleston but now resembled a cross between the slums of downtown London during the beginning of the industrial revolution and a horror scene from a steampunk novel.

Slop and unspeakable refuse littered the streets. I didn't see a thing that looked remotely modern. No cars, airplanes, cell phones, computers, parking meters, nothing. But that made sense if this was all a creation from Edgar Allen Poe's mind. He died in 1848 so he was limited to what he actually experienced or what his mind could imagine about the future.

"Holy Toledo," Charlie exclaimed while pointing behind me.

I turned and at first my eyes couldn't comprehend what I was seeing then my input neurons assembled the visual data.

Lazily floating low in the sky was an air ship that I had always envisioned after reading a steampunk novel. It was a giant grey oblong balloon shape with a strange colorful flag stretching across the side.

The top half resembled the Hindenburg with four chimney stacks and dark blackish grey smoke curling out.

Thick cables cascaded down from the massive balloon that secured a black metallic ship underneath. Large cannons pointed out of the sides of the ship.

"This is insane," I whispered over to Charlie. "Is this even historically accurate?"

"Hmm huh," was all Charlie could muster.

We continued walking on the outskirts of the city along the harbor until we came to a small dock. A swarmy-looking man with a greasy porkchop style mustache and incredibly pale skin stood in front of a sloop. He wore a tattered blazer, black slacks, riding boots and was smoking a long pipe.

He spotted us and ran over. "Mr. Dalton, Mr. Dalton," he exclaimed excitedly. "I done as you said and waited. I had to beat back a few of the scourge and riffraff but as you can see, your vessel is ready to sail. The captain is below taking his afternoon nap. I'll fetch him." He spoke in a strange magnolia drawl with hints of an Irish peasant accent.

The man ran off and I turned to Dalton, "Where are we going?"

Dalton pointed toward the evil-looking castle in the harbor. *Oh Goodie*, what horrors could possibly await us there.

I glanced over at Charlie who just shrugged. For a person who studied the paranormal and unsolved mysteries he didn't seem to be taking this all very well. But our fate was set at this point. We boarded the ship and a few minutes later the sloop was heading out to Poe's Castle.

I almost laughed when I heard Charlie nonchalantly ask the ship's captain, "Where you from?"

The captain looked straight out of central casting from The Titanic. He was an older gentleman with a thick, neatly trimmed white beard like Christmas snow from a Hallmark movie. He wore a crisp blue naval suit adorned with colorful medals and ribbons with a white captain's hat.

He certainly looked like the part of a sea captain except his eyes were dead black without a sign of pupils and a deep scar ran from his forehead down to his chin. Tucked inside his thick belt was a giant machete and a pair of muskets.

And, of course, there was a gold raven pinned to his lapel. It had a set of onyx-encrusted eyes and in its talons was a ruby heart, colored like it was bleeding. I then noticed that the pork chop moustache man had a similar raven pinned to his collar and even Dalton had one pinned to his breast pocket on his massive black trench coat.

"You ain't from around here are ya?" The captain answered, looking at us with a suspicious glare.

"You can say that again." Charlie answered.

"Try not to be such a smart aleck," I whispered to Charlie. "I don't think he's the sort of captain who'll let the woman and children off first if the ship starts to go down. You know what I mean?"

"So, where you from Cap?" Charlie repeated.

The captain looked out over the harbor. "I don't remember."

I stared at Charlie and we both knew what each of us was thinking—what have we gotten ourselves into?

"What about you?" Charlie asked the mustachioed man, who sat smoking at the helm.

"Best not know the answer to that one, boy," he laughed while blowing a large plume of smoke into the air.

I stared out across the harbor. The only thing that appeared tranquil in Dark Charleston was the water, although it was dark as molasses and, if you stared long enough underneath, it was churning, giving no indication of calm.

There was a lot of activity in the harbor with boats of all shapes, sizes and time periods. I spotted an old Chinese junk ship making its way toward the Ashley River. Sleek wooden canoes, hollow bodies scraped from oak trees. Fast moving Arabic dhows like the ones that carried spices through the Indian Ocean. Steamships spat black smoke into the air. Portuguese caravels from the Horn of Africa. Ships from dreams anchored or slowly moving to unknown destinations.

The captain steered toward Poe's Castle along the edge of what would have normally been Sullivan's Island. When we came around the bend a medieval stone castle appeared right on the sandy beach.

"What in tarnations is that?" Charlie asked aloud.

"That is Vlad Tepes Castle," the captain offered. "He rules the island. A bit stern some people say, but all-in-all, I'd say a pretty reasonable chap."

"Whose Vlad Tepes?" I asked the captain.

"In our world," Charlie chimed in. "His real name was Vlad Dracul III and he ruled a portion of Romania during the 15th century."

"Didn't he have something to do with Dracula or vampires or something like that?"

Charlie chuckled. "He's a cult figure with an interesting history. Dracul originated from the Latin word Draco meaning dragon because Vlad's family was a member of the prestigious Order of the Dragon. The Order of the Dragon was a chivalric, semi-military and religious society created in 1837 by the Holy Roman Emperor. The Order's main purpose was to defend the Catholic Church from its enemies, who at that time were the Muslim Turks who were constantly invading the Balkans. Vlad lived during the Late Middle Ages which was a period highlighted by calamities, upheaval, famines and constant war. Vlad's territory was in the center of a geopolitical storm because Eastern-Central Europe was in a constant battle with not only its own neighboring countries but with the Ottoman Turks who were hell-bent on conquering all of Europe. The collapse of Constantinople in 1453 had opened the floodgates and the Ottoman Turks mere making a relentless push westward with Hungary serving as the final line of defense. For Vlad that meant he was directly in the crosshairs of this battle between East and West and the cruelties inflicted upon his fellow man by both sides was barbaric.

Vlad was not a man to be trifled with and he was feared for his brutal, inhumane forms of punishment during his reign of terror. He ordered people skinned, boiled, blinded, decapitated, strangled, hanged, roasted, hacked, nailed and buried alive. He also enjoyed cutting off noses, sexual organs, ears and limbs."

"He sounds like a real sweetheart." I replied sarcastically.

"Ha. If you thought that was bad Vlad's very favorite form of punishment was impalement. In fact, he was so proficient in the torture that the Turks called him Vlad Tepes which translates to Vlad the Impaler. Vlad and his minions perfected the art of impalement, which was a slow, gruesome death. Thick stakes were sharpened to form a sharp point. The stake was pounded into the ground and then greased where unfortunate souls were placed on top of the sharpened end with the stake inserted into the anus. As gravity took hold the stake would slowly force its way through the body until the stake finally punctured a vital organ or the person just died from blood loss or shock. Unbelievably people could live for days before finally dying! During his bloody reign Vlad impaled between 40,000-100,000 poor souls. No man, woman or child were spared from Vlad's wrath."

"Gee sounds like a fantastic guy. Real southern hospitality. Maybe he'll invite us to his castle for lunch," I muttered. "Maybe he'll serve us shish kabobs. I still don't understand why you know so much about this guy?"

"Duh, Bram Stoker. He wrote the gothic masterpiece Dracula and with it the Vampire legend was born. Vlad Tepes was Stoker's inspiration and from his pen sprang Count Dracula. A night stalker who would leave his coffin at sundown to feed upon the innocent blood of the living."

"That's kind of cool. But I'm not going to that island under any circumstances. Dear god, look at that," I pointed toward the beach.

A swarm of seagulls were flocking in a mass near the beach in front of Vlad's castle. And when I mean a swarm, I've never seen anything like it. We're talking thousands and thousands of birds. A storm of mottled feathers, their horrific cries echoing around the castle. Gray plumage set loose in the wind. It was like an afternoon thunderstorm, except one made of scrappy gulls.

I now saw why the seagulls were massing on the beach. In front of Vlad's castle rows and rows of tall thick stakes rose out of the sand. Corpses in various states of decay were impaled onto the stakes. The wind suddenly shifted and the stench from the beach made me gag. I fought to hold back the hot, bile rising in my throat. The Captain and Dalton seemed quite unfazed. Yep, Vlad seemed like a nice guy alright.

I looked at Charlie. He was white as a ghost. Thankfully, the ship tacked away from the horrifying scene on the beach back toward Poe's Castle.

I slumped down on the deck with my head in my hands. I literally wanted my mommy.

CHAPTER 8

POE'S CASTLE

The captain docked the boat at Fort Sumter, or whatever the heck Dark Charlestonians called it. I guess Poe's Castle. The sound of the harbor slapping against the old brick wall surrounding the castle reverberated into the oppressive air. The dead spartina grass swayed like safety floats, which I should've taken as a warning sign. Horseflies buzzed through the air. Charleston sat like a mirage off in the horizon, appearing almost quaint and charming. Did I say almost?

Four soldiers greeted us. They stood at rigid attention, stern-faced, wearing what looked like old Civil War uniforms with ravens pinned to their lapels. Chillingly, their eyes were white and scarred, their faces cracked and sun-stained like old leather. They reeked of gunpowder and decay. The soldiers remained completely silent only raising their hands to their heads in quiet salutes.

"Let's go," Dalton ordered.

We followed him across the gangplank onto Poe's Island. The wood creaked beneath our feet and splintered in a few weak spots. I worried that we would fall straight into the churning, dark water below, probably riddled with waste and gunk and sharks and the ghosts of sharks. I definitely didn't want to become a shark snack, which should've been the least of my worries.

One of the soldiers approached and tipped his cap. "Good evening, Mr. Dalton," he said in quiet, raspy voice. "Mr. Poe has been anxiously awaiting your arrival. I am to escort you and your guests to his study at once. Please follow me."

The soldier led us across the grounds, stippled with holes and chunks of dead grass, and I was astonished at the detail of the castle obviously influenced by gothic architecture. The castle could've been something printed out of a travel guide.

In fact, it was so breathtaking that I almost forgot about being kidnapped at gun point and transported to an alternate dimension. The architecture reminded me of the Cologne Cathedral in Germany with its rib vaults, flying buttresses, pointed arches, stained glass, and monolithic black limestone.

Giant torches surrounded the exterior of the fortress with smaller ones positioned along the castle's walls so that it was well-lit despite the pitch blackness surrounding the island. The stone façade, though aged, was still breath-taking, each brick crafted one at a time, smoothed with careful hands. One by one by one.

I looked up at the enormous height of the structure and the flaming torches casting eerie shadows off the vast array of stone gargoyles, griffins, dragons and other beasts that had inhabited my nightmares since I was a kid. I shivered and side-stepped them.

We entered into a great room lined with enormous stained-glass windows allowing dust-stained light to filter down. The room was magnificent and would be a major attraction in my world. Glass chandeliers adorned with flickering candles, gold detailing along the walls, oil portraits of stern-faced women, their dark, haunting eyes following us as we moved through the building, but its beauty was tarnished by the horror that laid just outside the walls.

We walked through the great hall into a small passage. I almost felt like I should've taken off my shoes, feet tracking mud across the grand Turkish rug—a deep red, vermillion or crimson, garnet or merlot or sangria, something rich and unidentifiable, something regal, something rich as wine, something definitely belonging in a castle.

It felt like we were heading downward which should have been impossible considering the brackish water table, and I was not too terribly enthusiastic about the notion of drowning in an alternate dimension under a castle riddled with creepie-crawlies, ghosts, and quite possibly Mr. Poe himself.

I followed behind everyone as we treaded down a narrow, dimly lit corridor. The putrid smell permeated everything, making me nauseous. Sort of similar to the marsh mud, less refreshing though, filled with more decay, and devoid of the Atlantic breeze. A muted swooshing sound caught my attention causing me to stop in my tracks. A small door stood off to my right and a low almost inaudible humming came from within.

I knew I should keep up with the group. Getting lost in the catacombs of a creepy castle was not on my bucket list, but something was urging, almost forcing me to open the door. An invisible force, pushing me from behind. The sound emanating from the closed door was grating on my mind. It was maddening and melodic. It had a musical sort of cadence and yet, it was horrifically saddening to listen to. A cacophony of deep, low voices and I felt like if I didn't open the door, I would lose it and go crazy (and at this point, it was quite possible that I was already mad). I opened the tiny door and stepped inside.

Once again, the dimensions of the room should have been impossible, but I was catching on to the impossibility of it all. In fact, the notion of "impossibility" lost its meaning. What really was impossible at this point? The room stretched as far as I could see. In fact, I couldn't even determine where the room should have ended. A glimpse into a vacuum of space, cold and unending, nebulous and beautiful and absolutely terrifying.

I stood there in astonishment looking out at hundreds and hundreds of small wooden tables. Each desk contained a seated monk, all identically dressed in black robes furiously scribbling in large leather-bound books. Not one of them looked up.

However, when they lifted their quills, I could see a flash of their wrists, white and waxen like the melting candles in the great hall or the first sliver of a silver moon. Ink dripped off the tables in little puddles around their feet, catching the light of the candles, glowing on the wall. They were humming too. Like one large mass of insects with hive minds, deep guttural noises from the backs of their throats. I couldn't look away; it was almost beautiful, if not for their terrifying, blank faces.

What were they writing? The earlier madness in my mind had quieted some. I felt hypnotized and forgot about leaving the group when someone seized my shoulder violently turning me around.

"Best not to wander off, missy," the Civil War soldier replied flashing me a wicked smile, his yellow teeth glowing in the musty darkness. "There are things inside this castle that you best not encounter."

His words were jarring because the smile masked fear and he seemed afraid.

The soldier practically threw me back through the door, and after constant prodding from his rifle, we soon caught up to the group. Charlie gave me a 'what the hell are you doing' look. I just shrugged and mumbled that I would tell him later.

The dank passageway led to a series of stone stairs that should have led to the far tower. Although, I stress *should have*, since the interior of the castle defied all laws of observable physics. In fact, it seemed to occupy a plane completely separate from what I had existed in for eighteen years. This was quantum physics upside down, inverted, anti-reality. This was some real matrix shit.

I recalled the line from the movie: *The Matrix is everywhere. It is all around us. Even now, in this very room. You can see it when you look out your window, or when you turn on your television. You can feel it when you go to work, when you go to church, when you pay your taxes. It is the world that has been pulled over your eyes to blind you from the truth.*

Like I said, some real Matrix shit.

We climbed the winding stairs for quite some time when thankfully we reached the top of the tower. The lead soldier knocked on the door, paused, then opened it carefully, as if afraid it would creak too loudly.

We followed him inside. The room had high vaulted ceilings with giant candle chandeliers, casting muted light across the room, making our shadows grotesque, twisting up the walls as though we were morphing into the landscape itself. Creatures born from the innards of the castle, twisted and shadowy filled with a musty kind of darkness and dust that cast a muted light across the room.

An enormous banquet table was centered in the room with a lavish feast spread across it: the head of a pig, figs and apples, breads, meats, jams and sauces, flanks of lamb and goat, bowls of steaming lentils, rich red plums and cherries, platters of pomegranates, figs, dates, gold and silver chalices of fermented wine, the whole soiree lit by muted candlelight; and at the head of it was a man who was instantly recognizable.

He stood up and bowed slightly. "Welcome to my home. My name is Edgar."

"Holy Toledo," I heard Charlie mumble. "We really are in Alice in Wonderland now."

Edgar Allen Poe stood and walked over to us with a glass of dark red wine in his hand. He smiled, lips stained red, teeth filled with rot. In a leather overcoat and billowy white cotton shirt, mustache trimmed meticulously, a sharp pair of hazel eyes, the same color of the tortoise shell cat that sat in one of the velvet chairs.

"That is all for now," he dismissed the soldiers, leaving us and Dalton.

I'm sure I looked like a fool with my mouth agape unable to utter a word while Poe gave us the once over. He was quite the looker. Handsome, I guess, in a way. Poe must have understood what I was feeling because he gave me a crooked smile and said, "All that we see or seem is but a dream within a dream."

"Is this a dream?" Charlie blurted out.

"Maybe," Poe answered. "But if we are dreaming at least realize those who dream by day are cognizant of many things which escape those who dream only by night. Please, join me."

Poe smiled again and took a large swig of wine. I noticed that he too had a raven pinned to his lapel, but his was different from the soldiers, the captains, or even Dalton's. Poe's was bigger. It had a large set of silver wings, perched in mid-flight, encrusted with rubies and red diamonds. The beak of the great bird was open with a gold tongue unfurled from it, like it had paused in a shrill cry.

Poe motioned to the table where we all took a seat. Against the far wall, a fireplace ran at least forty feet from the floor to the ceiling, tall pillars of fire blazing inside. But it was what the fireplace was made out of that made me shiver. It wasn't constructed out of brick or stone. No, Poe's fireplace was made out of bones and skulls, thousands and thousands of them. Somewhere off in the distance, I heard faint sounds of chamber music.

A servant appeared out of nowhere and set down a glass of wine in front of everyone. I sniffed it and faked a sip, even though I was fairly sure they didn't have a drinking age in Dark Charleston. Dalton slugged his drink down in one motion, which was not surprising.

How do you begin a conversation with such a man? I cleared my throat and asked, "Mr. Poe, uh, it is nice to meet you. But, well, I mean—I don't want to seem rude, your hospitality being great and all and uh, the wine being incredibly delicious, otherworldly and well…" Again, how do you ease into a conversation with Edgar Allen Poe? "Do you have any idea where I could find my grandfather? I'd like to see him and take him back home. Please. And, uh, thank you?"

Poe curtly smiled. "Yes, of course. Joe is . . . occupied for the moment but you'll be reunited with him shortly. Your grandfather is a remarkably interesting man. He showed a tremendous amount of ingenuity to find his way here. I have enjoyed talking with him and learning about all the wonders of your world. The technology is mind numbing, positively hard to even grasp."

"Are you holding him prisoner?" Charlie blurted out.

Poe laughed and took a drink of his wine, viscous and red, a little dribbled down his chin. "Why would you say such a thing? After all, Joe traveled here by his own volition. Did he not?"

"That's true, but I heard him calling for help on his ham radio," I replied.

"Yes, Joe has told me about these things called radios. Quite fascinating. Your grandfather also told me about something called a cell phone. Do you have one?"

Charlie dug in his pocket and pulled out his cell phone.

Poe laughed like a child. "Astonishing. Please, contact someone. Let's see if it works."

Charlie hit a button and a second or two later I felt my phone vibrating in my back pocket followed by my trademark sci-fi ring tone. Typical, but which was embarrassingly applicable in the moment.

I pulled out my phone and accepted the call.

"Hello," I heard Charlie say across the table but not from my phone. The only thing I heard from my phone was an eerie static.

Poe laughed like a school child again, clapping his hands. "Marvelous," he replied.

"Well, it didn't really work, Mr. Poe," I replied. "The ringer seems to work but all I can hear is static on the line."

Poe waved his arm dismissively. "I do caution you that perhaps the voice you heard on that ham radio may not have been your grandfather. You realize that we are talking about two different worlds and in-between those worlds, is The Void. But The Void is not an empty vacuum as the name suggests, rather it is a world unto itself. A Never World that is the collective consciousness of all. It is the world where all dreams reside. How can you be sure that was your grandfather's voice? Even if it was… it is quite possible that it wasn't the version of your grandfather from your world."

I was having a tough time grasping the concept that Poe described, doubt creeping into my mind. A soldier entered the room and hurried over to Poe. He whispered something in his ear. Poe slammed his wine glass down and his genteel disposition faded into a look of madness. Pure anger. Like a switch flipping. His suave facade melted quickly off his face.

"I should have never trusted that scoundrel," Poe shouted, throwing a platter of the largest shrimp I've ever seen across the room.

"What is it?" Dalton asked.

Poe drank from his wineglass and almost immediately a charming smile fell back onto his face. "Blackbeard has sent his demands."

"And?" Dalton grunted.

"Well, he wants the usual accouterments those pirate bastards always demand—gold, ammunition, liquor."

"Easy enough," Dalton replied. "What else?"

Poe looked at me. "For some reason I cannot grasp, it seems he wants this young lady to deliver the goods."

"Wait," Charlie chimed in. "Blackbeard wants Alex to deliver the ransom?"

"Well," Poe raised his glass in a mock salute. "After all, it is her grandfather."

Then I understood the situation and rebutted, "Blackbeard is holding my grandfather hostage?"

"That is correct," Poe answered.

"How did Blackbeard take my grandfather as a hostage?"

Poe waved his hand. "Evidently, a few of his men somehow managed to sneak inside my castle and apprehend him. But don't worry the night watchmen have been punished quite severally for their lack of oversight."

Poe looked over at Dalton and they both started cackling like drunken crows.

"But no worries," Poe continued. "Blackbeard is ready to return him. And all you have to do is go fetch him."

"When do we leave?" I asked.

"First light."

"I don't like this one bit," Charlie whispered to me.

"I'm going with or without you."

"First light it is," Charlie responded to Poe.

"That's a good man," Poe answered jovially, sucking the fat off a chicken bone. "Anyway, I know you have had a long day of travels so my men will show you to your quarters for the evening. You will be safe inside your rooms. However, I must warn you that I cannot guarantee your safety if you were to leave those rooms during the night."

"Why is that?" I asked.

"Again, I don't have enough time to try and explain this world to you but let's just say, there are things that go bump in the night." And with that Poe once again started laughing hysterically, flashing a rotting smile at me and Charlie.

The soldiers reentered the room, bayonets in hand, and Poe stood. "These good men will show you to your quarters and I bid you a good night."

He left through a concealed doorway in the rear of the room and the soldiers motioned for us to follow them once again.

I looked at Charlie who cracked a tepid smile and said, "I always thought it would be cool to meet Blackbeard."

CHAPTER 9

ANNABELLE LEE

The soldier nudged me in the back with his rifle into my sleeping quarters. The door slammed and I heard a loud click. I tried the door handle; I was locked inside making me a prisoner.

The spacious room and décor made me feel like I was on a set of a Victorian period piece movie. The light from the oil lamps lit up a room alternating between a weird mix of the majestic and the macabre.

On the majestic side, there were tall ceilings with mahogany wood walls and exquisite oriental rugs. The bed was a grand four poster type with silk sheets and hand stitched pillows. There was a large stone fireplace that only the most talented masons could have constructed and hand carved furniture that would blow away the snootiest appraiser from Antiques Roadshow. I half-expected a silk night dress in a blush shade to be laid out on the bed, next to a pair of authentic pearl earrings and a bonnet. That was not the case.

Now for the macabre. There were no windows in the entire room making me feel claustrophobic and panicky. The candlelight made every object cast long, delirious shadows across the room with no windows for the light to escape. Paintings of all sizes covered the walls, and the subject matter was terrifying.

One painting depicted a fox hunt but instead of aristocratic gentlemen on horses with dogs and rifles in the countryside, the tables were reversed. In Poe's world a group of ravenous looking foxes chased an aristocratic man across a field. The painting next to it depicted the same foxes huddled around a fire with the aristocrat hogtied on a spit, slowly cooking above the flames.

Another painting appeared to be inspired from something out of Dante's Inferno. A demon or monster was in a large cave with naked humans scurrying around him with expressions of utter despair. The demon-monster had half a body sticking out of his mouth and in his hands he had dozens of mutilated bodies squeezed in his grasp.

I moved to the next painting. A flock of menacing ravens circled above Charleston while humans scurried in blind panic throughout the city. The painting reminded me of the Hitchcock movie The Birds.

That was it, I had enough of the artwork. I was more of a MOMA fan anyway. Modern art, being my forte, especially in that moment. All of a sudden, I couldn't keep my eyes open, and I stifled a yawn. Despite the fact I was trapped in a horrible alternative world I suddenly felt beyond exhausted. I just wanted to sleep. I managed to crawl onto the four-poster bed, and melted into the cotton mattress like it was the consistency of whipped cream. I pulled the down-feather to my chin, falling asleep before my head even hit the pillow.

A creaking noise woke me from my slumber. Before I had a chance to scream bloody murder, I recognized Charlie tiptoeing across the room.

"Jeez, Charlie! Are you trying to give me a heart attack? What are you doing?"

"Shhh," he whispered. "C'mon, let's check this place out."

I rubbed my bleary eyes. "How'd you get out of your room?"

He smiled. "In my line of work, you tend to break into a lot of things. I just reversed the process. Are you coming or not?"

I stifled a yawn. "I don't think it is such a great idea to be wandering around. Remember what Poe said?"

"I don't trust that bastard one bit," Charlie said dismissively. "You ever read The *Tell-Tale Heart*? He cannot be completely...together in the brain." Charlie tapped his temple for emphasis.

I slid back into the bed, so warm and soft, so similar to a marshmallow, perfectly toasted and gooey. I just wanted to go back to sleep and wake up from this nightmare.

"Okay, suit yourself if you want to be a lame'O. I'm going to check this place out."

He turned to leave and against my better judgement I jumped out of bed. "I'm coming but if I get bludgeoned to death by some gargoyle, I'm blaming you."

"I don't think a gargoyle would bludgeon you to death. Maybe just rip your face off and eat your intestines, but I will accept full responsibility."

"Gee thanks, that's reassuring."

Charlie peeked outside the bedroom door and motioned for me to follow him. We walked out into the dimly lit hall.

"Hopefully, everyone is asleep." Charlie whispered.

"Asleep?" Are you kidding me? We just magically slipped into some Charleston parallel universe and had a drink with

Edgar Allen Poe. What makes you think they even sleep here? Wherever or whatever "here" is?"

Charlie shrugged and cautiously started moving down the dark hall. I followed him like a puppy dog trying not to imagine what we might run into. A ghost. A demon. Michael Myers. The Headless Horseman. Lizzie Borden. Poe with unimaginable anger issues. Charlie grabbed a torch from the wall, and we walked for a few minutes down the never-ending hall.

"Hey," I whispered to Charlie. "Something's not right."

"I know," he replied. "This may sound crazy, but I think this place is constantly changing."

"What do you mean, changing?"

"I've noticed insignificant things at first, but they are increasing. Rooms are growing, passageways are shrinking. The light fluctuates in weird ways. Doorways are moving or disappearing. It's like the whole structure is alive and morphing into..." He didn't finish his sentence as a loud guttural roar echoed from somewhere deep in the castle.

Charlie turned and looked at me. "Now I'm scared."

"Should we go back to our rooms?"

We both turned to head back. "What the hell," Charlie exclaimed.

The hall we had just walked down was gone. Poof! Just like that, it had disappeared. We were facing a stone slab. Poe had warned us not to leave our rooms and now we were going to suffer the consequences.

We looked at each other. "Any more brilliant ideas?" I asked.

Charlies shrugged and I followed him the only way we could go at this point, forward, down a curved passageway that seemed to go on forever.

Finally, we came to a door. Charlie looked at me and I reluctantly nodded. He opened it and we stepped into a brightly lit room. Too bright to be from any natural light source. Where was the light coming from? Every square inch of the room was filled with paintings.

"What is it with the paintings?" I asked Charlie. "You saw the ones in my room, right? Poe must be a connoisseur of demented fine art or something.

"Yeah, my room had the same kind of stuff."

Charlie pointed to a painting in front of us. "I recognize this one. This is a famous painting from the late 1800's called the Isle of the Dead. Poe had died decades before this painting. How'd he know about it to be able to recreate it?"

I shot him a "how the heck should I know" looks and stared at the oil painting. A rowboat was transporting a coffin across a rocky inlet to an island covered in a grove of tall, dark cypress trees.

"Do you notice anything strange about the painting?" Charlie asked.

I squinted my eyes. "No."

"In the original painting the oarsman is supposed to represent Charon, who in Greek mythology ferried souls to the underworld. In the original, the oarsman's back would be facing you and you wouldn't see his face. Look more closely."

I walked closer to the painting. "Oh my gosh! Poe is the oarsman."

A noise from just outside the room almost caused me to pee in my pants. Someone or something was coming down the hall. The shuffling noise was getting louder. Whatever or whoever it was, it was getting close. I looked around but there was nowhere to hide. We both froze.

I held my breath as a ghastly shadow passed in front of the door. My heart was pounding so hard that I couldn't catch my breath. I looked at Charlie who had turned a whiter shade of pale.

The dark shadow passed, then a figure dressed in a loose-fitting white dress with a shawl draped around her shoulders stopped in front of the door. She wore no shoes and had shimmery black hair falling past her shoulders. The ghastly woman appeared to be in her early twenties. She turned and stared directly at us. Eyes vacant, almost translucent. It felt as if she was staring right through us. After what seemed like an eternity the woman turned and continued slowly shuffling down the hall.

We looked at each other with a collective sigh. Charlie tip-toed to the door and peeked his head out. He motioned to me and we left the painting room following behind the Ghost Lady who appeared to be in great distress or emotional agony. Like a teenage girl whose heart was broken by her average "insert name here" boyfriend who dumped her after a date at the diner where they shared a chocolate milkshake and a medium fry, and he still made her pay for it. Geez, I thought I had suppressed that memory.

Suddenly, she started repeating lines that sounded like they came from a story or a song:

"Of my darling—my darling—my life and my bride,
In her sepulchre there by the sea—
In her tomb by the sounding sea."

Charlie grabbed my arm. "I think I know what she is saying."

"What?"

"I think she's reciting lines from a poem by Poe called Annabelle Lee."

"Annabelle Lee?" I repeated.

"Yeah, it was one of Poe's last poems. It's about his love for a beautiful young lady who died. You're not going to believe this, but I think that's Virginia Clemm."

"Who's that?"

"She was Poe's wife. They were first cousins, and they were married when she was only 13. She died in her early twenties of what they called consumption or what we now call tuberculosis. A lot of historians believe the story Annabelle Lee was based on their marriage."

"Holy Moly! Should we call out her name?"

Charlie shrugged and in a faint voice called out, "Virginia."

She stopped dead in her tracks and turned. Pain etched into her face, and I was no longer afraid of her, I felt sorry for her.

"Why?" she painfully addressed us. "My husband, sweet Edgar. Why did he summon me to this place? Why has he entrapped me here, condemned me to be neither alive nor dead. Why Edgar, why? Every night he summons me to dance on the ocean, but I am cold, so cold."

I felt bad for her. Like really bad. This was definitely worse than my "boyfriend" milkshake incident and consequent dumping. I wanted to give her a hug and buy her a pint of Ben and Jerry's Cookie Dough Ice Cream or something.

Virginia Clemm aka Annabelle Lee turned and continued to shuffle down the passageway quietly reciting the lines from Poe's poem Annabelle Lee.

"What should we do? Should we follow her?"

"What else are we going to do," Charlie answered. "We can't go back the other way."

We followed behind her for a brief time. "Hey look, she just went into a room down there," I whispered to Charlie.

We ran up to the doorway. There was no sign of her. She had disappeared into thin air.

Charlie pointed to the far corner of the room. "Look, there is a door in the floor."

We rushed over. Charlie turned the handle and lifted up the door. A spiral suitcase wound downward from the floor. I peered down and immediately felt an overwhelming sense of vertigo. I got dizzy, my palms grew clammy and sweaty. I could feel my body start to wobble. Charlie must've sensed it and grabbed hold of me.

"Are you all right?"

I took a deep breath. "I'm okay, I think it was just the height. It's not too often I've opened a door in a floor with an endless staircase. How far down do you think it goes?"

Charlie peered over and whistled. "It goes straight down as far as I can see. I can't see the bottom."

"Any sign of Virginia?"

He shook his head. "Do you think you can make it down the stairs?"

I gulped. "Ah, well... I guess. But why don't you go in front of me and promise me you'll catch me if I pass out."

Charlie smiled weakly. "You'll be okay."

We slowly started down the spiral staircase. I couldn't see the bottom although I was trying my best not to look down. We circled downward for at least five minutes when a little doorway appeared off to the left of the staircase.

Charlie turned back toward me. "You want to continue down or should we see what is behind the door?"

I took a quick peek down and I still couldn't see the bottom. "I'm thinking the door option."

Charlie maneuvered over to the edge of the stairwell and opened the small door. He crouched down and climbed through the doorway. He held his hand out for me to follow. I grabbed it and was pulled through the doorway.

I had seen this before. Rows and rows of monks sat at little writing tables furiously writing in leather books. I couldn't believe it! We were back in the room that I had wandered off into when we first entered Poe's Castle.

CHAPTER 10

PLUTO

We stared at the bizarre sight of endless rows of monks still hovering over small desks furiously scribbling in large leather-bound books. Their waxy faces were masked by hoods with hands moving like quick, gray birds. Just like before, they didn't acknowledge our presence in any way.

The collective shrill from their quilled pens was driving me crazy. I can't explain it, but it reminded me of a dentist drilling into a tooth with the noise reverberating inside your brain. Only this was a hundred times worse.

"What do you think they're doing?" I asked gritting my teeth.

Charlie looked around the room. "I have no idea. And I'm not sure I even want to know."

Not one of the monks glanced up from their frenzied work. "Do you think they are in some kind of trance?" I asked. "Like a spell?"

Charlie shrugged. "Who knows, but let's get out of here before we find out."

We gingerly made our way through the endless rows of desks expecting one of the deranged monks to spider monkey attack us at any moment.

Lining the walls were giant wooden bookshelves, stretching to the ceiling, housing thousands of books, bound in taut leather with ambiguous wax gold dates branded along the spines. All slid into neat rows. The candles burned. The quills scratched. The monks wrote.

We finally passed the last row. We had reached the end of the room, and there was a door. An exit out of this madness but into what new mayhem would it lead to? I really did not want to fathom any of the possibilities, any of the other mysteries lurking in the shadows. I almost raced past Charlie because I couldn't get out of this room fast enough.

"Hold on." Charlie walked back toward the last monk's desk. He peered over his robed shoulder looking down at the book.

My anxiety level was exploding by the second and I couldn't take it any longer. Charlie's stupidity was going to get me stabbed in the back with the point of a monk's quill (not the way I expected to go in Dark Charleston, especially with the notion of an evil pirate ransoming Grandpa Joe).

I tapped him on the shoulder. "Let's get the heck out of here."

He waved an arm and continued peering down at the monk's book. I was about ready to sock him in the head when I caught the eye of one of the monks. He was sitting a couple rows away from me and it had happened, recognition.

I froze, mid-punch, shocked that he had stopped writing but more so by his eyes. They were glassy, pale, and cold, like the surface of a frozen pond. I couldn't look away. Most of his face was hidden by his hood, but I thought I could see his lips curl into a smile. It wasn't evil or demonic and his teeth weren't sharpened into points, but it still sent a shiver through my spine.

He grabbed a tiny scrap of parchment, dipped his quill into a pot of dark green ink, and resumed writing. Then he folded the parchment and held it over the candle that burned on the corner of his desk. It caught fire and slowly burned, the smoke trailing down the side of his desk like dripping water. The smoke vapor spread over the floor passing over my feet. The monk lowered his head and once again scrawled into a giant leather book. My clenched fist fell to my side. That's it, the heck with Charlie. I high tailed it to the door.

I opened the door, and a gust of cold, dank air greeted me. Thank God, it was a hallway. The door slammed shut behind me and I turned to see that Charlie was right behind me.

Much to my relief the mind-numbing shrill had stopped torturing my brain. "Nice going nitwit! I hope you got a good look at what that demented monk was writing because you almost got us trapped in there, in another dimension. You could've led us to the stupidest death fathomable."

Charlie didn't respond and his eyes looked weird, almost vacant.

"You okay?"

After no response I shook his arm. "Charlie," I repeated. "Are you okay?"

It took a few more aggressive shakes before he snapped out of it.

"Huh," he mumbled.

"Are you all right?"

"Yeah. I think so."

"What was the monk writing?"

"The present."

"What?"

"You remember when Dalton said that this is Poe's world, and he is in the process of creating it through his imagination?"

"Yeah."

"Well, I think the monks are a manifestation of his mind and they are literally writing the reality of this world in real time."

"What was written on the page you were looking at?"

"It was about us. Before I left to catch up with you I watched him write:

The smoke vapor spread over the floor passing over my feet. The monk lowered his head and once again scrawled into a giant leather book. My clenched fist fell to my side. That's it, the heck with Charlie. I high tailed it to the door."

We heard a big meow followed by the appearance of a large black cat from around the corner. What an odd little creature. It stumbled through the darkness, crying out softly.

"I don't like cats, "I heard Charlie say. "They're bad omens."

The cat slowly approached us. At first, I thought it was wearing a loose collar but as the cat got closer, I saw it was actually a miniature noose tied around its neck. Even more disturbing, one of its eyes was missing, revealing a hollow socket.

The cat came up to me and rubbed against my leg. I didn't know whether to pet it or kick it. It meowed again and my animal lover instincts kicked in. I crouched down and rubbed its head.

"Hey buddy. How's it going?" I cooed. "Aw, look Charlie! He's cute!"

Charlie grimaced. "He doesn't have an eye."

"We've slipped into an alternative horror dimension and your freaked out by a cat?"

"I don't like cats or clowns, okay."

"Aw! How's it going, buddy?" I continued petting the cat.

"To be honest with you, not so good," the cat answered.

I instantly stood up and looked at Charlie in shock.

"Did that cat just talk?" Charlie asked incredulously.

I looked back down at the cat who was staring up at me. I wondered if the regal purple walls contained arsenic or something hallucinatory drug, because I was definitely losing every semblance of reality.

"My name is Pluto," the cat continued. "And in case you are wondering Master Poe dug out my eyeball and hung me from a willow tree. He likes to do that every couple of days when he gets in a fit of rage if his stories are not progressing as he desires. And if you don't mind, could you please remove the noose from my neck?"

I reached down and took the noose back off. "Why would he do such a thing"

"Because his soul is black and tortured."

Poetic, I thought, followed by poor kitty.

Charlie coughed. "I think I know, um . . . this cat's history."

"Please share," Pluto replied. I thought I heard a hint of sarcasm in his voice but then again, it was a cat. I always imagined, if they could talk, they would be snarky, sardonic, and condescending.

"Well," Charlie continued. "Poe authored a short story titled *The Black Cat*. It is about an animal lover who descends into alcoholism and perverse violence. He begins mistreating his wife and his black cat, named Pluto."

"Hmm, that is a weird coincidence," the cat replied. "Since we just also happen to be in Mr. Poe's home and my name is Pluto."

Charlie looked at the cat suspiciously. "One night Pluto attacked the man after being abused one time too many. In a fit of rage, the man seized Pluto, cut out one of its eyes then hung it."

"Are you connecting the dots yet, Mr. Wizard?" Pluto asked.

Charlie gave Pluto an annoyed look. "I'm starting to," Charlie said in exasperation then looked over at me. "Did I just respond to a cat?"

I shrugged and he continued, "After killing the cat that night, a fire destroys the house, leaving him in dire poverty. He later adopts a one-eyed black cat that he finds at a shady tavern, but after he nearly trips on the cat, he attempts to kill it as well. When his wife intervenes, he kills her instead and hides her body inside the walls of the house. In the end the black cat reveals the narrator's crime to the police."

Pluto must have approved of Charlie's interpretation because it meowed loudly and rubbed up against my leg.

"That is an awful story Pluto," I said while reaching down to pet him. "Is there anything we can do for you?"

"I would be much appreciative if you take me with you when you leave. I find it monotonous, not to mention quite painful, to be tortured by that lunatic every couple of days."

"I promise you Pluto, I'll take you with us. But we are trapped as well. We can't even find our way back to our rooms."

Pluto's tail bobbed up and down. "Follow me, I can get you back."

Instead of trailing Charlie, I now found myself being led by a talking cat named Pluto that had been conjured from one of Poe's gruesome stories.

We followed Pluto through a maze of tunnels before the cat finally stopped in front of our rooms. "As promised, your sleeping quarters," Pluto replied.

I sighed in relief. "We can still get a few hours of sleep. Hopefully, Poe will never know about our little escapade."

Charlie yawned. "Let's hope. I'll see you in the morning."

I opened my door and Pluto followed me in. He jumped up on a cushioned chair and curled up in a ball, purring loudly. His one eye stared into the dark: glassy and cold.

I crawled into bed and once again fell asleep.

Chapter 11

Blackbeard

A hissing noise woke me from my slumber. I had absolutely no clue what time it was, though I wasn't even sure if time existed the same way as it did back home. For all I knew, I could've aged 50 years in my sleep and was now stricken with arthritis and a love for early-bird dinner omelets.

At some point in the night, Pluto must've crawled in bed with me because his tail was swooshing against my face, and he was hissing.

I rubbed my eyes. "Hey buddy, what's wrong?"

Pluto hissed again and that is when I spotted a soldier standing at attention at the front of my bed. He had the familiar blank look with vacant eyes.

"Jeez, you ever hear of knocking?" I asked pulling the sheets up to my neck even though I was fully clothed.

"Mr. Poe has requested your presence for breakfast," the soldier responded with no emotion. "I will wait outside to escort you."

He then turned 180 degrees and marched out of the room, slamming the door behind him. I sighed. Maybe I should talk to Poe about proper etiquette for his house servants.

I slid out of bed and pressed down the sleep wrinkles on my clothes. I was putting on my shoes when Charlie knocked then entered my room.

"You ready?"

"Yeah." I looked back at Pluto on the bed. "Don't worry buddy, I'll come back and get you."

Pluto stared back lazily, completely unconcerned, a sliver of his white eye shining in the early morning.

The soldier led us down a series of twisting hallways and through a tunnel which somehow led us back to the large banquet room that Poe entertained us in last night.

And sure enough, there was the man of the hour. He was sitting exactly where we left him last night. And he was still drinking wine. Did this place make people immune to alcohol? Did he ever sleep?

Last night's feast had been cleared and replaced with a morning banquet: platters of fruits, loaves of bread, porridge, ham, quail's eggs, and slabs of bacon.

Poe snapped his fingers, and a soldier refilled his chalice with more wine. He looked waxen in the morning light, dank and filtering through the windows like the remnants of a thunderstorm.

The far wall had an enormous window cut out of the stone and I could see Charleston's harbor, filled with dozens of boats, zeppelins swimming through the air like baleen whales, silent, casting large shadows on the surface of the water. It was almost beautiful. If not for the horrors in the city. If not for the fact that we were about to negotiate for my grandpa's release with the world's most fearsome pirate.

Blackbeard, written into history books as an angry, dirty buccaneer who stole the 40-gun French warship called Queen Anne's Revenge and wreaked havoc in the Caribbean and along the east coast before launching a blockade on Charleston. Like I said, it was almost beautiful.

"Alas, my friends have come back," Poe exclaimed cheerily. "I hope you had a restful night. Are you hungry?" He plucked a few grapes from a crystal bowl and carefully placed them in his mouth.

"We're good and we are ready to go," I answered because at this point I just wanted out of this abominable castle. I was willing to take my chances with Blackbeard.

"Splendid. Your transportation awaits. And remember, your grandfather gets sent back to me after Blackbeard gets his ransom goods."

"And what did Blackbeard want in exchange for Grandpa?" I asked.

"Funny you would ask that. You would think scourges like Blackbeard would want the usual pirate items: women, liquor, gold, guns, blah, blah, blah. But no, not this one. For some reason, these things do not amuse this pirate. He requested literature, musical instruments, a fiddle, mandolins and concertinas. Along with silver flatware and a chess set. I have no idea what he wants with this stuff, but it is not my concern. My concern is that you'd better keep your end of the bargain and return with your grandfather. So, listen closely, if your grandfather is not in my castle by sunset tomorrow the consequences will be quite severe."

"Don't worry, we'll bring him back. But there is one last item, and it is non-negotiable— I'm taking Pluto with me."

Maybe it wasn't the wisest decision to make a demand with the man who was largely responsible for any semblance of safety I had in Dark Charleston. But I had promised Pluto, and I didn't really want to steal him from Poe. Stealing seemed unwise. Stealing seemed like certain death.

Poe refilled his wineglass. "And why may I ask would you want that mangy thing?"

"I love cats," I answered.

Poe took a sip of wine. "So be it. I have no use for that miserable creature. You know he bit me the other day?"

"Hope he doesn't have rabies," I goaded, secretly hoping that Poe might get some of his own medicine.

"Damned thing!" Poe struck the table and laughed. "I can see that miserable cat foaming at the lips! You're doing me a favor!"

He smiled, sincerely. He seemed child-like, clad in a black cloak, the edges of his collar turned up, his mustache barely there. In that moment, I thought about his revered death. A cold, rainy morning in October. Poe found face down in a gutter. The last of his days spent racked by hallucinations and delirium.

Poe glanced up at me, the raven pinned to his lapel shining. He smiled, slightly. It wasn't vindictive or evil. It wasn't masking a conniving scheme or fictitious. Poe lifted a finger to his lips, still staring at me, snapped his fingers at the nearest soldier, indicating our departure.

As we turned to leave Poe called out, "Remember, this is my world. If you run, I'll track you down. If you hide, I'll find you and if you double cross me . . . Well, you do so at your own peril. And Miss Alex! Don't say I didn't warn you! Pluto can be a real pain in the rear!"

We followed the soldier out of the room and could hear Poe talking, "But he's quite nice in the winter!"

"Why do we have to take that dang thing?" Charlie grumbled. "I'm allergic to cat dander. You think they have any Allegra here?"

"They don't have electricity you idiot. I doubt they have over-the-counter allergy relief."

We didn't have to go far to find Pluto. Like a shadow, obviously unamused by Poe's banter, he was right outside the door.

I picked him up. "You sure you want to go with us? You know we're headed to a pirate's ship."

"Any place is better than this nightmare," Pluto answered.

"Okay then. Off we go."

We followed the soldier out of the castle where a sloop loaded with Blackbeard's ransom goods was waiting for us. I was shocked. The treasures in the boat were eloquently crafted, carved from fine wood and metal and stone.

Charlie whistled, obviously impressed. "These should be in a museum!" He gestured at the chess boards, tea sets, fine China, and paintings.

Despite my misgivings, I was going to be reunited with my grandfather. After that, I had no idea what was going to happen or how we were going to get home but at least I found him.

We hopped into the sloop along with two soldiers and a captain who sailed us across the harbor. We sat in silence, alone in our thoughts. I looked back toward Charleston. I saw thin trails of smoke curling up from half a dozen spots in the city. What was daily life like in Dark Charleston? Was everyone like the soldiers, mere puppets without any real thought or control over their lives? Just functioning and not living? Were they happy? Miserable? Did they even know the difference?

A steam-punk zeppelin slowly drifted across the city and the inner harbor was bustling with shipping activity. The water was calm, but I still couldn't get over how gloomy everything appeared. It was morning and there were no clouds, yet a pall seemed to hang down enclosing everything in a thick grey light.

I turned and stared out into the end of the harbor that emptied into the Atlantic Ocean. Anchored against the horizon was Blackbeard's pirate ship—the infamous Queen Anne's Revenge.

It looked like the quintessential pirate ship from the movies except that it was massive with cannons sticking out of every port. A tattered black flag whipped about in an almost nonexistent wind. I could make out a few pirates scurrying about the ship. This was about to get real interesting.

As we approached the ship, netting was flung down to us followed by a band of pirates. In a mad rush they started grabbing the chests of ransom goods and hauling them back up the ship. They completely ignored us.

Once all the goods were unloaded, we heard a voice call down to us. "Good morning my dear friends. Welcome aboard the Queen Anne's Revenge."

I placed a hand over my eyes to block out the sun and a tall, striking figure came into view. He had long black, neatly trimmed hair that matched a thick beard. He was dressed in fine clothing. He wore a black vest with gold buttons over a white silk shirt with ruffles at the wrist. His black buccaneer pants had fitted cuffs just below the knees and he wore a pair of shiny black leather boots. A large cutlass dangled off one hip with a bandolier of ivy-gripped pistols strapped across his chest. He displayed a laid back, reserved but confident expression.

"I am Edward," he continued. "We have much to discuss. Please come aboard."

"Who's Edward?" I whispered to Charlie.

"I think that is Edward Teach."

"Who the heck is that?" I whispered back.

"Blackbeard."

Okie dokie. I was surprised by his countenance. Half-expecting a scurvy-ridden monster of a man with no moral compass and an unstoppable sense of vengeance. I had some difficulty climbing up the netting because I had Pluto in one hand, and he didn't help much.

Blackbeard grabbed my free arm and gently helped me onboard.

He bowed. "Miss Alex, I am pleased to formally make your acquaintance."

"Nice to meet you as well, and this is Pluto."

I sat the cat down and Blackbeard looked down at him with amusement. "Welcome aboard my friend," he addressed Pluto. "You are just what we need aboard this ship. There are enough mice, rats and other vermin aboard to keep you feasting for more than nine lives."

Pluto rubbed up against my leg then happily ran off, perhaps looking for breakfast.

"This is my friend, Charlie."

He held out a hand to Charlie. "My pleasure good sir."

I watched them shake hands. This was not the pirate displayed on TV or in books. I expected his face would be craggy and weather beaten but instead he looked like he hadn't toiled a single day in harsh conditions. He acted more like a professor at a Vermont liberal arts college than some blood thirsty 18th century pirate. It seemed surreal and it felt like he would lead us to a cramped office where he'd be grading essays by candlelight, shelves filled with leather-bound first edition books, cracked spines but otherwise in pristine condition.

Blackbeard's small crew stood off to one side in the background. Blackbeard may not have resembled his historical reputation, but his motley crew did. They looked like the homeless of the seven seas. Most of their tattered clothes hung limply from their thin frames. Unlike Blackbeard, their faces were weather-beaten and gaunt. Most had sores covering their arms or faces and their hair was a tangled greasy mess. One pirate forced an evil grin, revealing a few discolored, jagged teeth and receding gums. They all looked like they suffered from scurvy and were in desperate need of limes and penicillin shots.

"We have delivered the supplies from Mr. Poe," I continued. "I think the arrangement was for me to take my grandfather back to Poe's Castle after delivery."

"All in due time my fair lady. For his safety he is aboard another ship not too far from here. He is being accompanied by my dependable partner, a gentleman if you should know, the honorable Stede Bonnett. Anyway, it is custom for new arrivals to join the captain in his quarters for a meal. But I give you my word that your grandfather is safe and after lunch I will take you to him."

What choice did I have. "Okay, thanks for the hospitality."

"Of course," Blackbeard answered. "And now, let's indulge ourselves with brunch."

We followed Blackbeard to the stern of the ship and down a small flight of stairs. His quarters were at the back of the ship, and they were nothing like I expected. I felt as if I had been transported to a luxury suite on the Titanic rather than a rat infested, smelly, pirate ship.

The walls and ceiling were a dark mahogany with light colored cypress hardwood floors. Two windows with, of all things, bright flowery curtains brought in natural sunlight. A small bed sat in the corner with a large table pressed up against the far wall. A handsome desk was in the other corner and bookshelves lined the far wall. And yes, there were actual books in them. (My prediction not being too far off after all in regard to the liberal arts professor).

The table was set for lunch, and it looked like a royal extravaganza. In the center of the table a small roasted pig was set on a large serving platter. A basket of oysters, plates of shrimp, loafs of sweet-smelling breads and fruits of all sizes and varieties was spread around the table.

"Wow, this looks incredible. You sure you don't want to share this with your crew? They look a little emaciated."

Blackbeard laughed. "I appreciate your concern for my crew. But rest assured, they are fed appropriately."

"Doesn't look like it to me," Charlie interjected. "They look like they're half-starved to death."

"It is of no concern of yours. They are zamboids."

"Zamboids?" I repeated. "You mean zombies?"

"I am not familiar with zombies. They are zamboids."

"What's a zamboid?" Charlie asked.

"It means they have been reconstituted in physical form but their free will, their spirit or soul if you want to call it that, never crossed over. Think of them as ghosts who go on living though they are closer to the dead than the living. They are like animals in that they function. They owe their miserable existence to that fiend Poe who conjured them up in his hideous monk's room."

"Hmm . . . since you brought that up," Charlie chimed in. "Didn't Poe create you as well? Why are you not a zamboid?"

Blackbeard let out a great laugh then flashed a serious, slightly diabolical expression toward Charlie. "That is a reasonable question. Poe was responsible for bringing me here. That is true. But he cannot control me. My free will is too strong for that alcoholic derelict. That is Poe's great flaw, his ego. He thought he could create a world with strong willed, powerful people like me and Vlad Tepes, Hannibal, Caesar, Cleopatra, Genghis Kahn, Galileo, Alexander the Great, Shakespeare, and many others. He thought that these people would be his play toys and would bow down to him like dogs. But what he didn't understand is that like a hurricane, you cannot control these people. They are forces of nature. Their minds are too free, too strong to be ruled by a demented drunkard like Poe. He has lost control of his world, and he is desperately trying to seize it back. His last stronghold is Charleston and soon that will also fall."

Pluto had followed us into Blackbeard's cabin and began purring at my feet.

"I still don't understand what this has to do with my grandfather?" I interrupted.

"Poe's incarnates is limited to the knowledge of his world past and present. Your grandfather is, other than you, from the future and he came here on his own. Poe believes that he possesses knowledge, technology that will give him an advantage and help him defeat his enemies. And also help him create a world from the future."

"And that is why you stole him from Poe?"

"Yes."

"Then why are you going to give him back to Poe?"

"I didn't say that did I?"

My 'Houston we have a problem meter' shot through the roof.

"I said that I would reunite you with your grandfather," Blackbeard continued. "And I will. Trust me if you love him you don't want him to go back to that scoundrel. No good will come from it and ultimately your grandfather will pay a terrible price for his association with Poe. It was a trap; he was never going to let you, or your grandfather return home."

"But what about Poe? Won't he come after us?" I asked.

Poe didn't seem entirely like a villain. In fact, he seemed rather eloquent. Of course, slightly insane. But then again, he abused cats, and he did send a deranged cowboy after us.

"You let me worry about Poe. Our forces don't want you here. Rest assuredly my fair lady, my objective is to send you back to where you came from. What you don't know is that if you were to venture a mere 40 miles in either direction of Charleston, you would be bathed in bright sunlight instead of this constant gloom that has settled upon this place like a curse. Poe is getting desperate because he's trapped. I control access to Charleston by the sea. Hannibal and Alexander's armies are amassing in the east and Vlad Tepes is leaning toward joining us, which would box Poe in for certain. But enough of this for now, let's eat."

I suddenly felt famished and reconciled that I was nothing more than a dandelion in the wind. Controlled by forces that I had no power over.

I sat down and dug into the feast. Charlie must have also been starving because neither one of us said a word except to pass a plate. We ate and listened as Blackbeard entertained us with jovial banter, describing the political affairs of Dark Charleston, the scandals, the historical figures lurking in quaint beach bungalows, the operas he attended, the classics he had read, the languages he studied, the chess games he played with emperors and kings and queens, the poets he met, the artists he visited.

It was stunning that the world's most notorious, vicious pirate was, in fact, a Renaissance man.

When we finished I asked Blackbeard again, "Okay, you promised, let's go get my grandfather."

"Charlie, are you a gambling man?" Blackbeard asked, ignoring my question.

"That depends."

"Well, per my word I will take you to Alex's grandfather, but I have a proposal. I need to run a quick errand and it would be more advantageous to me if we did that before we reunited Miss Alex with her grandfather. I propose a little wager. I will play you one game of chess and if I win, we run my errand first, after that we can fetch Alex's grandfather."

"That was the original agreement anyway," I protested.

"Right you are. So how about I sweeten the proposal for you? If you win: We leave immediately to get Grandpa Joe and by word of honor, I'll grant you full protection and a safe return home. And on top of all that you can choose any treasure aboard my ship as an added bonus."

Charlie glanced over at me with raised eyebrows. "Can we have a second to discuss?" Charlie asked.

"Certainly."

I didn't like where this was going. I stood up and followed Charlie to the end of Blackbeard's room.

Charlie whispered into my ear, "Look, this is a good deal either way. I know Blackbeard seems all refined and gentlemanly but don't forget he is a pirate. It may be best to keep on his good side. Let's humor him with the wager. We really can't lose. If he wins, we run a quick errand. We'll still get your grandfather. But if I win, we get Joe, Blackbeard's sworn protection and treasure. Anyway, you have nothing to worry about; I am an expert chess player. I led my high school team to the state quarter finals, and I still play online all the time. There is 0% chance I can lose to an uneducated 18th century pirate. I guarantee it."

I sighed. He did have a good point about our options. "You're such a geek. Wait a second. You said quarter finals. You didn't make it to the finals?

"That was my teammates' fault. I won my match. Trust me this is a layup. I guarantee it!"

"Okay. Just win the dang game so we can get my grandfather."

Charlie smiled. "No problem."

Five minutes later I said to Charlie, "Good playing Einstein. How could you lose in seven moves? That is almost impossible."

"I, uh…." Charlie mumbled.

"The chess gambit is called the Legal Trap," Blackbeard interjected. "You fell for one of the classic blunders of chess. Even 'worse than getting into a land war in Asia.' I sacrificed my queen while positioning minor pieces to set the trap. You fell for it completely and all that was left was checkmate. Ha! You never knew what had hit you. The strategy is named after a dear friend of mine, the French chess master Sire de Légal."

I gave Charlie a disgusted look. "You are an idiot."

Chapter 12

Vlad Tepes aka Dracula

Once again, I found myself in a sloop sailing to a place I definitely didn't want to be. A commonality in every single event following the moment Dalton showed up at the Charlie's apartment door. This time we were headed to Sullivan's Island.

Normally, Sullivan's Island is a cutesy little tourist island with a strip of stores (ice cream parlors, cafes, pubs, a smattering of retail stores and offices) filled with locals and tourists. Normally, rows of colorful bungalows, nestled along the Intercostal, and, of course, beaches, people laid out on bright towels, fishing and crabbing from the shore. Unfortunately, we were not headed toward Sullivan's Island, the cutesy little tourist town. Oh, no. Definitely not. Too mundane. Too enjoyable.

Instead, we were heading to the beach of a thousand impaled corpses and a rendezvous with the real-life Dracula.

This place was far from the tourist attraction and the melting Cherry Garcia ice cream cones and the yacht rock radio station and the nice, gentle tide and the boaters and the surfers.

Nope, we were meeting a man from the dark ages called Vlad Tepes. Yikes! Even his name sounded scary—like some sort of disease. Neither of which were remotely comforting.

We sailed across the harbor and thankfully came ashore downwind and out of sight of the beach carnage. Though you could still catch a whiff of the stench bearing a reminder of what was lurking on the north side of the beach. Charlie looked green. I wasn't sure if he was seasick or if it was the smell of rotting corpses or a combination of both. He managed to hold it together and we disembarked onto the beach.

We hiked a beach trail across sand dunes for about a quarter mile arriving at Vlad's Castle. It looked like any typical Romanian—slash—Transylvanian medieval-slash-Dark Age castle from your worst nightmare. Horrifying.

I suddenly missed Poe's lodgings, where there was a certain… elegance. A *je ne sais quoi*. Though gothic in nature, and terrifying to admire, it had more of a cathedral feeling, church pews and stained-glass windows, the ruins of what once was an amazing feat of architecture hidden in an English or Swiss countryside with a clean river nearby, ivy growing along the back walls, and flowers in the garden.

Vlad's castle, simply put, was like hell incarnate.

Two massive stone gargoyles stood on each side of the wooden door leading inside the castle. We followed behind Blackbeard and as we approached, I nearly jumped out of my skin. When we neared the door the gargoyles suddenly came to life and lowered their spears blocking our entrance.

Their stone bodies groaned which sounded like bits of rock being pulverized as they moved. Really, the sound was more like laughter, a gritting-back-of-the-throat kind.

Blackbeard didn't even flinch. He abruptly flung their spears upward and yelled at the heinous beasts, "How many times do I have to tell you dumb flying buzzards to keep those things out of my face? You're lucky I don't stick both of you on one of those giant toothpicks your master is so fond of. Vlad is expecting us. Let us through."

The gargoyles were ugly things, stony-faced and angry, but their eyes held a glint of onyx mischief. And though I don't know if they completely understood Blackbeard's threats, but the monsters slowly lowered their spears and then metamorphosed back into stone pillars.

Blackbeard knocked loudly on the door. I wasn't completely sure of castle etiquette, but this seemed much too casual of an arrival.

He turned around to us. "Whatever you do never enter a vampire's castle uninvited."

Dark Charleston etiquette. But isn't it supposed to be the other way around? I thought a vampire always had to ask a human permission to enter their home. But what do the movies know? What do I even know?

After a few seconds, the massive door creaked open. An eloquent man appeared from behind the door. He was short and stocky with a long straight nose and large wide green eyes. His face was clean shaven except for a wide mustache that ran across his entire face. He possessed long black hair with thick curly locks that fell down to his wide shoulders. He was dressed in fine clothes that I imagined noblemen of his time wore: a red velvety overcoat, a silk button-down with black pants and leather boots.

He bowed slightly and in a genteel but heavy Eastern European accent replied, "Please, enter. You are most welcome into my home."

Charlie nudged me, snapping me out of my dilemma about proper vampire etiquette. "C'mon space cadet. Let's get this over with."

We stepped inside and I swear the temperature dropped twenty degrees. We stood in the foyer. The floors, walls, and a high vaulted ceiling made from dank, discolored stone. A few bats flew around the vaulted ceiling.

I wish I had packed some garlic. I longed for Poe's elegant foyer and hearty feast. Even the soldiers, with their vacant eyes and sharpened bayonets and less than human countenance, were more inviting.

"Vlad, let me introduce you to Miss Alex and her traveling companion Charlie. They come from the future world."

I noticed Vlad's eyebrows subtly rise up when he heard the word "future."

"Welcome." Vlad gestured around the room as if enlightening us about some matter.

Vlad quickly turned back around to face us, opening and closing his mouth like a goldfish, like he wanted to say something but couldn't find the words. Finally, after a few seconds of blubbering, Vlad spit out, "Blackbeard has told me that your world has painted me in ... how should we say ... a less than heroic light?"

"Here we go," I heard Blackbeard mumble under his breath.

"Evidently, I have learned that your history books suggest I was a blood-thirsty tyrant," Vlad continued. "I've heard words bandied about like bloodthirsty, evil, wretched, beyond cruel and murderous. Is this true?"

Poor Vlad looked pained, embarrassed, and a little morose. His face tightened into an expression I couldn't quite interpret. Anger, not really. Fear, definitely not. Sadness, a hint. No, it was a misunderstanding. He didn't understand his legacy in our history books.

I felt even worse for him when I realized that I'd never heard of Vlad Tepes before and had no idea what he was even talking about.

But luckily, Charlie answered, "They say history is written by the victors. I'm sure history has misinterpreted you to a degree. But remember your name has lived on for centuries and you have inspired generations through literature and movies. You are the man behind the Dracula legend. In my world, people love vampires and even admire them."

Vlad appeared to appreciate Charlie's comment and commented, "Inspiring you say? I understand that is good. Inspiring. Written into history. Yes . . . yes, very good."

"I wouldn't worry too much about it, Vlad," Blackbeard interjected. "You should hear what they think of me in the future world."

"Your reputation is well-deserved, Blackbeard," Vlad spat. "I serve God through the noble and chivalrous Order of Dragons. I fight to serve God first then to protect my lands and people. You, on the other hand, serve only your best interests and insatiable lusts. Pillage, pillage, pillage. Burn, burn, burn. That is all you are interested in."

An ironic outburst considering the state of Vlad's beach. I chose (wisely) not to interject.

Blackbeard sighed like a parent trying to ignore a bratty child for the hundredth time. "How many times have we been over this Vlad? Stop being so darn sensitive about what they write about us in some other world. But in my defense, at least I am not a hypocrite who hides behind his gods to justify his atrocities to mankind."

I looked over at Charlie with a smirk. They sounded more like an old bickering married couple than two of history's most notorious bad guys. Even Charlie appeared to be enjoying their banter.

Finally, Vlad broke the silence with a hearty, albeit disturbing laugh. "You pirates are really interesting characters," he said in a more relaxed tone. "I would like to have been around in your days. Please follow me. I know time is of the essence and we have matters to discuss."

We followed Vlad up a flight of stairs to a cavernous room that looked eerily similar to Poe's. Did these guys have the same interior designers I wondered? Probably so. I mean how many interior designers could there be in hell. Three large trunks sat on top of a large banquet table in the middle of the room.

"Please have a seat. Shall I send for some liquid refreshments? Anyone hungry? I have some wonderful game hens or boars that can be slaughtered and cooked up lickety-split?"

"I'll pass on the fowl," Blackbeard replied. "But a glass of your mead would be splendid."

Then he turned towards us, "You must have some of Vlad's special Dark Ages Honey Mead. It is exquisite. I've tried hundreds of times to duplicate it but can't. The bastard refuses to give me the recipe."

"Sure, I'll have one," Charlie piped in like an excited kid who just got front row tickets to the circus.

"Do you have any water?" I asked, parched from the unusually salty harbor, the wind and the hike.

Vlad looked at me quizzically and asked, "Do you need to clean yourself? I can fetch a chamber maid to draw a bath if you wish."

"No, I'm good. Just water would be fine." I replied wondering why Vlad was suddenly worried about my hygiene. I doubt they have deodorant in this world and I started to get a little petrified that I was beginning to smell?

Vlad looked over at Blackbeard with an equally confused expression.

"I know this sounds crazy Vlad," Blackbeard interjected. "But evidently, future people actually consume water. Real liquid water."

Vlad looked almost disgusted. "And they don't perish?"

"Evidently, no."

"Astonishing. I have never purposely drunk water before," Vlad added pondering this fact before changing the subject. "But just so I understand, why does your world consider a man of God such as I, a man devoted to the care of his people and a humble servant to Jesus. Why does your world consider me nothing more than a murderous servant of the devil?"

Blackbeard sighed, I guess unsurprised by Vlad's singular track of mind. He gave us an exasperated look. "As you've probably gathered, Vlad is very concerned about his reputation. And he seems to have a one-track mind."

I looked over at Charlie who replied, "Well, Vlad most future people don't believe what they read anyway. And I understand the period you lived in was, well, very different than mine."

Vlad pounded the table with his fist. "I've been surrounded by enemies on all sides my entire life. How'd you like to live like that? But yet, I refuse to serve anyone else except for my people and God."

"Here we go . . ." Blackbeard mumbled.

"My family's name Dracul originated from the Latin word Draco, meaning dragon. We are members of the prestigious Order of the Dragons. A chivalric and religious society created by the Holy Roman Emperor to defend the Catholic Church from its enemies, mainly the Muslim Turks who were constantly invading the Balkans. My army was the last defense from these spawns of Satan. I have been sanctioned by the highest officials in the Catholic Church to defend our civilized lands and I am absolved in any suffering that may result in that defense. I am doing God's work. I fear not, for I will be rewarded in heaven."

Blackbeard stood up and pointed to the chests. "All right, Vlad. We get it. You're a hero. A saint even. Not to change the subject but actually to change the subject, we've got to go."

Vlad stood and seemed to relax a little. "Of course, As we discussed, here is your offering. When do we destroy Poe and his satanic creations?"

"Wait a second," I replied to Blackbeard. "I don't care what plans you two have cooked up. Our deal is that you bring us to my grandfather and then we go home."

"Of course, but we need protection to get to Ocracoke Inlet where your grandfather is waiting. Vlad is going to help us with that. He and his soldiers will accompany us to Ocracoke and then you shall be reunited with Grandpa Joe. After that, our plans will be of no concern of yours. But first, I have a favor, and this is non-negotiable."

"How can a favor be non-negotiable?" I asked.

Both Vlad and Blackbeard both burst out laughing. "These future world people obviously don't understand the concept of a favor."

"No, they don't," Vlad added.

Charlie and I just gave each other a flabbergasted look and Blackbeard continued, "Yes, this is a different world than yours but what if this is just your world's new past and what if in a couple hundred years our two world's timelines intersect."

"I have no idea what that means," I said.

"I need you to help me hide these chests in a secure location that won't be found by anyone or destroyed by Mother Nature."

I looked over at Charlie and his expression was exactly what I was thinking. This guy was playing us like fools but what options did we have? I honestly was beginning to doubt that we'd ever leave Dark Charleston. We were nothing more than pawns on Blackbeard's ivory chess board controlled by a force larger than ourselves. Maybe Charlie and I should conspire. Plan a way to locate my grandfather. Sneak back to

Dark Charleston. Find an escape. Even as I was thinking this, I knew it was an entirely implausible scheme. I knew that one foot in the wrong direction and I'd probably end up impaled on Vlad's beach or stuck in one of Poe's dungeons.

Blackbeard smiled because he knew what I surmised about his plan. "The loot in these chests is for a rainy day. You never know our world's timelines may cross and this would help me get adjusted."

"Should be plenty of money," Charlie said. "And adjusted for inflation you'd probably be a billionaire."

"What is inflation?" Blackbeard asked.

"I'll explain later," Charlie answered. "Trust me, what you have is enough. I can even recommend a financial advisor if you like. I'd guess he'd recommend a conservatively balanced portfolio of stocks and bonds. But I'd also advise investing in real estate, precious metals, private equity and alternative investments like commodities."

"Shut up, Charlie," I chimed in because I didn't care one bit about the money. I just wanted to go home and if Blackbeard decided to tag along, well that was someone else's problem not mine. He'd give a heck of a pirate tour to the tourists.

"We'll discuss this advisor matter later," Blackbeard replied. "So, what do you think, Charlie? Where should we store this?"

Charlie thought for a while before replying, "I can't account for the cross dimensional changes or time warps between Dark Charleston and Normal Charleston, but I know a place that has stood the test of time. But first we have to see if that hiding place even exists here. Obviously, Blackbeard, I can't guarantee anything."

"I understand. Now Vlad, I trust you and your soldiers are ready to travel to Ocracoke?"

"It is arranged."

"And again, why is Vlad coming to Ocracoke with us?" I asked, not too happy about these developments.

"Protection Miss Alex. Poe has scripted British warships. We are at war. But don't worry, my spies have told me we have a few days. We'll hide the goods and I'll get you reunited with you grandfather with plenty of time to spare."

Somehow I felt like I'd heard this story before. Maybe being in Dark Charleston was like a time loop or like that movie Groundhog's Day, with the day replayed and slightly altered each time. What a way to live out eternity.

We left Vlad's castle. I was still dying of thirst because I never got my glass of water.

CHAPTER 13

FORT MOULTRIE
AND SIR ISAAC NEWTON

We hiked back across the dunes with Blackbeard and a few of his pirate zombies or zamboids, as they were called locally. They were slow-moving with sunken eyes and pale skin as if plagued with a kind of grotesque, medieval disease like bubonic plague or leprosy.

The blank-faced zamboids carried the treasure chests and never uttered a peep or a complaint. I felt sorry for them in a way. They were mere puppets in this theater of the absurd. Their strings being pulled by the likes of Blackbeard, Vlad and Poe for their own personal exploitation. Still, I didn't think now was the time to interject for humanitarian aid.

I turned to Charlie and even though I had an idea I asked, "Where are we headed?"

A wry grin flashed on his face. "Back to where we started this adventure."

Yep. I was right. We were heading to Fort Moultrie. "How do you know the fort even exists in Dark Charleston?"

Charlie shrugged. "Trust me. I just have a feeling."

"I hope it isn't that same feeling you had when you played Blackbeard in chess and guaranteed victory."

"Ha. Ha." Charlie laughed. "This time is different."

"Yeah right, if I had a dime for every time I heard that I'd be rich by now."

"You'd have a few shillings and maybe I'd have a bit more dignity," Charlie retorted.

"Shillings?" Vlad and Blackbeard heads turned suddenly at the mention of money. Charlie just shrugged and I wondered if even in Dark Charleston money was the root of all evil.

I looked around at my surroundings and it was weird hiking across the sands of Sullivan's Island with no houses, signs, speedboats, paved roads, or beachgoers. No preppy real estate agents named Jolene trying to sell prime inlet plots with chocolate chip cookies. No retirement-aged men with a passion for metal detectors. No dropped ice cream cones. No Lily Pulitzer mothers toting around their sandy toddlers. Nada. Only the endless expanse of sand, the sounds of the ocean and a sky filled with swarms of birds.

I wondered how many different versions of Charleston existed. Could there also be different versions of me running around in other strange worlds? Maybe worlds inhabited with aliens or dinosaurs or creatures my imagination couldn't even fathom?

Or is it possible that after we slip into the subconsciousness of our dreams, we escape the boundaries of our current world and are able to catch glimpses of ourselves in other dimensions? Could this all be some really long, strange dream?

My internal thoughts dissipated when we came around a large dune and Fort Moultrie appeared. It was mortared, surrounded with artillery, standing like an armored giant. It was even more magnificent in Dark Charleston. A true, stone fortress.

"For once, I guess you're right," I needled although this version of Fort Moultrie looked much older than the one I remembered. Much more gothic, weathered and beastly.

"Of course, I am. But it was an easy call," Charlie admitted. "Poe was stationed at Fort Moultrie when he was in the army and as we know his story *Gold Bug Island* was set in Charleston. It makes perfect sense that the fort would be here, even if this world is a manifestation of his imagination."

"It looks real enough to me but what if there are soldiers stationed at the fort?" I asked. "They may not take too kindly to us especially if word got out that we double crossed Poe."

"Hmm. I didn't think that far ahead."

I looked at Charlie and began thinking I really needed to stop letting him make the major decisions. Blackbeard held up his arm and motioned for us to stop. We crouched down in the sand and surveyed the surrounding area. There were no soldiers, only a solitary figure seated on a bench in front of what looked like an apple tree. Which was strange because apple trees didn't grow in Charleston. There was also a large table next to the bench and the man seemed completely transfixed in whatever he was working on.

Blackbeard stood back up. "We're good to go. I know who that is, he is called Newtie. He won't bother us. Now the question is, where exactly do we hide all this?" He glared over at Charlie. "And remember, I'm holding you responsible for the safety of this."

"Me? I not sure that I'm the one to trust with this," Charlie protested.

Blackbeard clapped him in the middle of the back. "Bollocks, my boy. You've seen both forts in both Charleston's. If anyone knows a good hiding place it would be you."

Charlie sighed. "Okay. Well, the reason I thought the fort might work is because it has survived for hundreds of years in my Charleston. It's a national monument so no condo developers or city planners or road crews can dig or tear it down. The point being that hopefully, you won't have to worry about someone accidently digging it up."

"I have no idea what you are talking about, but it sounds good to me," Blackbeard exclaimed. "But we need to be quick. Our time is almost up, and we need to get back to the ships."

"Who is Newtie?" I interrupted.

"Oh, just some mad professor or scientist or whatever. He's harmless and won't bother us a bit. He's completely crazy in my opinion but I've been told he is one of the smartest humans to have ever existed."

I looked over at Charlie and I knew we were thinking the same exact thing. We made our way to the fort's entrance and the man had moved to the table, which was filled with manuscripts, books, maps and scientific equipment. He still hadn't noticed us or bothered looking up from whatever he was working on.

"Newtie," Blackbeard called out in a loud voice. "Any luck with your quest to find the Philosopher's Stone?"

The gentleman finally looked up acknowledging our presence. He appeared frazzled, hunched over parchments filled with archaic text, and his white hair aged him. He wore a smart pair of wire glasses and squinted up at us.

"Edward, nice to see you again good sir. I am close, so remarkably close. The answer eludes me for the time being, but I know the questions, so it is just a matter of time."

Blackbeard gestured grandiosely with his arms. "Let me introduce Miss Alex and Charlie."

The disheveled man stared over at us and bowed his head. He was like a ruffled kind of bird, perched on the bench, pecking at his book with the dulled nib of his ink pen. His eyes swiveled over us. From me to Charlie to Blackbeard back to me and Charlie. He extended a hand, covered in black ink. "Pleasure to make your acquaintance. I am Sir Isaac Newton."

"Ah, Newtie! So formal today, aren't ya?" Blackbeard laughed.

"Hello," I managed to say because I was standing in front of one of the greatest minds the world had ever known. Here was the man who had discovered the composition of white light, gravity, laws of motion, calculus and who was the father of modern physics. And he was right here in Dark Charleston as if he had been peeled from a page of one of my high school textbooks.

"What are you working on?" Charlie asked.

"Do you know how gold is created?" Newton asked flipping through his pages.

"Um, I know it's dug out of the ground," Charlie responded. "And that it is worth a lot of money."

"Yes, but the arbitrary monetary value humans place on it is not important. The question you should be asking is how is it actually created?"

"That I don't know," Charlie answered.

"Well, think about this the next time you hold a gold coin or ring in your hand. Gold is a naturally occurring element with the symbol Au and an atomic number of 79. All gold in the universe is created in nature from supernovae explosions. The abundance of gold is about 0.005 parts per million making it one of the rarest elements in the earth's crust. All gold atoms are formed in the center of suns. After billions of years a small number of these stars of a certain mass may explode into a supernova which are the most intense and violent explosions in the universe. Only in a supernova is it possible to create atoms with 30 protons, 40 protons, 50 protons or even 60 protons. Nature prefers even numbers for stability, but every so often, the star will forge an odd-numbered atom, a real rarity—Gold! Gold is a rare, odd-numbered atom with 79 protons. For every single gold atom in the universe, there are 1 million iron atoms. After the supernova explosion a few gold atoms are then cast out into the universe where they float around in empty space for eons. Eventually, some of these gold atoms may join a cloud and some of these clouds may eventually condense into a planet like earth. Gold is not formed inside the earth because it is an inert element. Most of the gold that has been discovered in the mantle and crust was brought to us from outer space as a result of a supernova explosion. All the gold ever mined in the history of mankind would fit inside this fort."

"Wow, I never knew that. That is pretty cool," Charlie exclaimed.

"What type of research or experiment are you doing out here?" I asked wondering if one of the greatest minds to ever exist was a Gold Bug.

Blackbeard interjected, "I plunder for my gold, but Newtie is trying to magically create it."

Blackbeard turned so his back was to Newton, wide-eyed, and gestured around his head, suggesting Isaac had lost a few marbles. He stood suddenly and raised his palms to the sky. Blackbeard suppressed a smile.

Newton grew agitated and replied sternly, "Not magically. Supernovas are God's creation, and the universe is a machine. A machine of his design and creation. Through the science and art of alchemy if I can discover how to turn a base metal into gold, then I can discover the designs of God's wonderful machine. And then we can understand the true nature of God."

I wrote a paper on Newton in high school and during my research I discovered there was another side to Sir Newton. He was obsessed with alchemy, the occult and the apocalypse. Bit of a whack-a-doodle you could say. He believed that science and religion could coexist, and that invisible spirits inhabited the world. Even though he is known as one of the world's greatest scientists, his quest for knowledge ventured into less scientific avenues. He poured over ancient manuscripts looking for clues to the designs of the universe. He was also obsessed with the bible, in particular the Book of Revelations and was convinced that there were secret codes in the Bible. He scoured ancient languages obsessed that their writings would allow him to predict the future. Newton went so far as to construct a floorplan of King Solomon's temple that he claimed was a template for esoteric knowledge. In his lifetime he handwrote over a million words by hand on the subjects of alchemy, bible studies and the occult.

"It was a pleasure meeting you," Newton continued.

"And I wish I had more time to visit but I must return to my work." He pushed his spectacles up and began to pour over his text.

"He's lost a few marbles," Blackbeard muttered.

We said our goodbyes and entered the fort. As we walked in an overwhelming sense of déjà vu hit my system. Every neuron in my body was exploding like an electrical grid during a power surge.

I stumbled and Charlie grabbed a hold of me. "Alex, are you okay?"

I was struggling not to pass out when the strong sensations abruptly subsided.

"Alex, you okay?" Charlie repeated.

I took a deep breath. "Yeah, I just . . . I can't explain it. It was like a combination of intense deja vu while sticking a finger into an electrical socket."

"It's just this fort. I've got a weird vibe as well. I think this place, no matter what world it is in, is a beacon or a transistor or a gateway to parallel universes."

"This area is on a powerful ley line near the bloodline of the world, the 33rd parallel," Newton called out from behind us.

I stared over at Charlie who said, "See, even in Dark Charleston, the 33rd parallel holds significance."

I shrugged my shoulders, and we caught back up to Blackbeard and his merry band of zamboids.

"Aren't you worried about Newton out there?" Charlie asked. "He could be following us or at the very least he knows that you're hiding something important. Aren't you afraid he will take it after we leave?"

Blackbeard looked back toward Sir Newton. "He knows there is treasure including gold in these chests, but he is not a concern to us or the treasure."

"How so? I mean his greatest quest is trying to magically create gold out of thin air. You don't think he may want to pilfer your gold?" I asked.

"He is governed by much different laws than us," Blackbeard scoffed. "He is not interested in possessions or physical wealth. He lives for only one thing and that is knowledge. And wealth and knowledge are two vastly different things."

"I guess that makes sense," Charlie replied. "Okay, so historically, in our world, this fort has survived hurricanes, the Revolutionary and Civil Wars and endless development. There was a book called The Secret where the author gave clues to where he had buried actual treasure at different sites throughout the United States. There were a lot of treasure hunters that thought Fort Moultrie was one of the recipients of that treasure. I did a lot of research. I don't think Fort Moultrie was one of his spots but based on that research I know a spot that will stand the test of time no matter what world we are in."

"Enough dilly dallying, son. Just point the way."

Charlie stopped his rambling and led the crew to his hiding spot. The zamboids dug two gigantic holes, set the chests in and covered them back up. And I do have to say Charlie's hiding spot was ingenious. Even Blackbeard seemed satisfied. After we finished securing Blackbeard's treasure we bid farewell to Sir Newton and headed back toward Vlad's castle.

After Blackbeard got a little way ahead of us Charlie whispered to me. "Hey, if we ever get back to Charleston we could be rich."

"What do you mean?"

"The treasure. If our worlds are somehow dimensionally interconnected, when we get back home we can dig it back up. Who knows, it could already be there. Waiting for us to claim it."

"First, let's focus on the task at hand, getting home. And second, do you really want the wrath of Blackbeard hanging over you for the rest of your life? Or the lives of your doppelgangers in alternate worlds?"

Charlie ignored my concern and continued rambling, "The first thing I am going to do is buy a new car. Then, take a vacation to Scotland. Probably upgrade my apartment, buy some new furniture. You know, living above a Subway isn't exactly luxury. I could upgrade and live above East Bay Deli or at least a Jimmy Johns or Firehouse Subs. I could also buy a portfolio of blue-chip stocks and income-producing bonds and …"

"Okay, JP Morgan," I interrupted. "Like I said, let's just worry about getting my grandfather and getting home."

"Yeah, you're right. But I know one thing for sure, I'm buying season tickets to the RiverDogs baseball games no matter what."

I ignored Charlie as he continued rattling on about how he was going to spend his millions as we hiked back to Vlad's Castle. We passed by two pirate ships anchored about three hundred yards offshore.

Blackbeard turned back toward us. "Transportation has arrived. Feel free to board either ship but if I were you I'd hitch a ride with me. Until this world, Vlad had never even seen the ocean. Lucky for him I put a few of my men on board to actually sail the vessel and keep him out of trouble."

From down the beach we heard a high-pitched scream and turned to see a well-dressed man who seemed oddly out of place come running down the beach.

"Edward…Edward… wait," the man screamed.

He ran up to us then doubled over trying to catch his breath.

"Well, what is it my good sir?" Blackbeard snapped. "Spit it out."

The man managed to catch enough of his breath to stand up and address Blackbeard. "Edgar Poe has commanded a ship and plans on rendezvousing with Lieutenant Maynard and his British war ships in two days' time. They plan on attacking you near Ocracoke Inlet."

"The battle continues," Blackbeard casually replied then shoved the man down to the sand. "Come on you two."

We followed Blackbeard down to the water's edge and the waiting rowboats, then we were ferried out to the ships. We once again boarded Blackbeard's ship and began the journey up the Carolina coast to Ocracoke Island.

Chapter 14

Ocracoke Battle

We lazily sailed through the day with light winds and a calm sea. The water was ominously clear and still, like staring through glass and I oddly longed for its dark churning. For once nothing extraordinarily strange happened except I had an uneasy feeling one of Blackbeard's zamboids was watching me.

He never got close but every time I turned in his direction, he was obviously spying on me and would turn away pretending to be working. I asked Charlie about it, and he said he'd keep an eye on the man, but he didn't think too much of it.

I guess Charlie was right because as the hours passed I lost track of the zamboid and didn't see him for the rest of the day. That night we slept on the top deck underneath the stars and even though on the surface all was calm we knew a storm in the form of Poe and the British war ships was brewing. Thunderheads in the form of artillery and gun smoke.

I had trouble sleeping despite the calm and, instead, listened to the water lapping against the hull of the ship until I finally drifted off to sleep.

The next day broke cool and misty. The sun cast a dirty shadow across the sky. I woke stiff as a board, no pun intended, and saw Charlie staring out on the horizon.

I got up, stretched my sore body and walked over to him. He pointed out in the horizon and replied nonchalantly. "Looks kind of strange."

"What does?" I answered.

"The horizon. I mean I know what the ocean's horizon is supposed to look like but check it out. I'm I crazy or doesn't it look like some type of a weird mirage?"

I squinted my eyes and stared out as far as I could see. I hadn't noticed it before, but Charlie was right. There was an eerie "haze" or "shimmering" at the farthest point of sight. Was it just a trick of light and distance or was there something more to it?

"You're not crazy. It looks like the light is being distorted or reflected or, I don't know. It would be interesting to see what is on the other side of this ocean."

"You mean if we turned course and sailed due east would we run into a Dark Europe or Dark Spain or Dark Africa?"

"I guess."

"Well, in the real-world Poe never ventured across the Atlantic so my guess is that he hasn't created those places, yet."

"It's probably only a matter of time."

"Yeah. I don't know, if he hadn't created it maybe we'd just sail off a cliff into some unknown abyss. Or maybe it is just an endless ocean."

I took a deep breath. "This is all so weird. I guess any possibility is a probability, just like a vast ocean in an infinite universe. Or maybe this world is flat like a pancake and eventually we'd sail off the edge into oblivion. Or maybe, a

Dark Europe or Africa does exist, and is filled with monsters that we've never dreamed of and maybe…"

"Okay…okay," Charlie interrupted. "You're thinking too much, not to mention you just said 'maybe' a thousand time."

"Maybe you're right," I laughed.

But I couldn't shake the view of the horizon. It was simultaneously peaceful like soft static coming from a radio or the tail end of a nice dream. But underneath a violence was building that could erupt at any moment.

"Good morning," Blackbeard interrupted our brainstorming session about the possible horrors from beyond. He was dressed to the nines in an elegant white shirt and a black coat with a tail that nearly trailed to the deck. He wore a silk hat with a long feather of some exotic, unfamiliar bird sticking out of the brin of his hat. His eyes shimmered and his beard was neatly trimmed. "What a fine day. And soon, Miss Alex, you will finally be reunited with Ol' Grandpa Joe."

I bit my tongue to stop myself from making an off-color comment because I had heard that story before. Still, Blackbeard looked assured and confident.

"How far away are we from Ocracoke?" I asked.

"We should be at the inlet in the next couple of hours depending on the winds. You sure y'all don't want to stay around for the battle? It should be a dandy. Brimming with glory."

"No offense," Charlie answered. "But in our world you did not fare too well in that battle."

"Yeah, you might say I lost my head," Blackbeard replied letting out a great roar of laughter.

We both looked at each other and joined in with his laughter because Blackbeard had been decapitated in that battle in our world. It was funny that he could joke about his own demise in such a callous way.

In pirate folklore, after suffering dozens of sword and gunshot wounds, Blackbeard only succumbed when a British soldier snuck up from behind and decapitated him. The story went that Blackbeard's headless body had been thrown overboard and his body swam a few laps around the ship until it finally sank into the depths of the ocean. I truly hoped he would fare better in this battle. I thought he was a rather genuine person, and I was a good judge of people.

"Charlie, I could use someone who has his wits, unlike these dang zamboid fools. You don't appear to be a yellow belly. Why don't you join us in and experience the glory of a naval battle? And don't worry, I have no intention of losing to that scoundrel Lieutenant Maynard and his lackey's this time around. I have a fool proof plan in place.

"Hmmm. Thanks for the vote of confidence but I'll have to pass this time. I gave Alex my word that I'd help her get her grandpa back home and I'm beginning to miss my Wednesday meatball sub from Subway. But I hope you're right and you can rewrite history. Well, at least here."

"You can always change something. Anyway, look around my boy, do you think history from another world applies to this place? I'm not going to be rewriting history; I'm going to be creating it!"

"He's got a point," I said, nudging Charlie in the ribs.

"Anyway, the last time at Ocracoke I was tricked. But since you're so caught up in history did you know I was given a pardon by the North Carolina governor?"

"Really," Charlie answered.

"Absolutely. I was promised safe passage and as such, I was not expecting to be viciously attacked. History is always written by the victors, but the Virginia Governor and that British hypocrite Maynard conducted an illegal raid by attacking me."

"I didn't know that part," I admitted. "What was the battle like?"

"Oh, it was magnificent. I commanded two ships: *The Queen Anne's Revenge* and *The Adventure*. The British scallywags had the war ships: *The Ranger* and *The Jane*. Their commanding officer, Maynard, was a cunning bastard for sure. We were at a huge manpower disadvantage, but we still put up a valiant fight. And of course, as you know, the rest is history. But this is my chance at redemption. I was double crossed last time, and I would still have outdueled those bastards if I didn't have a bunch of cowards surrounding me. Now, I've got the upper hand. I've got a crew of dimwits for sure, but they are fearless zamboid pirates, not to mention Vlad and his fanatical vampire crew. It will be utter destruction for Maynard and Poe's forces."

"Hey, wait a second," Charlie cut in. "I just thought of something—what if Poe is killed? What happens to this world?"

"What are you talking about boy?" Blackbeard asked defensively.

"Well, Poe created this world. If he is killed does this place, I don't know, just disappear?"

"Charlie's got a point," I interjected. "Who knows what would happen. Maybe you should just try to capture him."

Blackbeard appeared to mull our concerns over for a few minutes like he was contemplating the taste of Vlad's Medieval honey beer.

Then, Blackbeard's eyes darkened, clouding like the morning sky. "That is easier said than done in the heat of battle. I can't control vampires, zamboids, and pirates in a fight to the death. We'll just have to take our chances. After all, if we all go puff because Poe is killed, so be it. I'm not too worried. We'll just end up in another world, a new adventure."

Blackbeard began cursing at a zamboid pirate who was throwing hunks of bread up to a flock of seagulls. "Excuse me, I have to get these fools back to work. As you can see their attention span is about a nanosecond and we've got work to do."

We watched Blackbeard leave and we both looked at each other. "Nanosecond?" I said to Charlie.

Charlie shrugged. "Where in the heck did he hear that term? Because obviously, it shouldn't be in his vocabulary."

"Maybe there is a Blackbeard in the future, and they have become entangled."

"Entangled? What's that mean?" I asked.

"It is a weird physics theory. Entanglement simply means that if two entangled particles, like say photons, were separated and sent in opposite directions, they could be hundreds of light years away from each other but despite the vast distances if you did something to one of the photons like say spun it, the other photon would instantly spin as well."

I shook my head. "Which would mean one of the most basic laws of physics, the speed of light, is wrong?"

"I guess you could say that but that's above my pay grade. I'm just saying maybe the Blackbeard in Poe's world is entangled with a Blackbeard from a different multiverse and that Blackbeard uses words like nanoseconds."

"Okay Einstein, you're making my head hurt. But what if Poe is killed? Maybe he has created some kind of failsafe and instead of this world going puff, what if we find ourselves trapped in some other abomination that is even worse than here?"

"Well, let's just plan on being long gone when that happens. Let's get your grandpa and skedaddle out of here as fast as possible."

I hoped Charlie was right. Maybe Poe was some kind of immortal being in Dark Charleston. Like his writing couldn't be unwritten, woven into the narrative like some undying malevolent entity.

I couldn't worry about that possibility anymore, so I watched the crew prepare for the upcoming battle for the next couple of hours and late in the afternoon we sailed into Ocracoke Inlet with Vlad's ship just behind us.

Dead stalks of seagrass floated like rafts and bobbed in the ship's black wake. I could see land, but it was bare and sun-bleached. Dead, leafless trees stretched out of the ground like white fingers. We anchored next to Stede Bonnet's ship and prepared to board.

I had made it. It was finally happening. I was going to be reunited with Grandpa Joe!

CHAPTER 15

CALM BEFORE THE STORM

All three of Blackbeard's ships were tied together, behemoth wooden beasts, with gangplanks thrown across for access between the vessels. It looked as if they were being tamed, the way the ropes crisscrossed between. I anxiously stared at Bonnet's ship trying to spot Grandpa. Its black flag whipped ominously in the wind.

"I don't see him," I said to Charlie.

"I'm sure he's somewhere. He may be below. Heck, he probably doesn't even know we're here."

"I hope you're right."

I watched the chaos as zamboids stumbled back and forth, scurvy-ridden, casting oil into the ocean from buckets, hoisting thick ropes, fixing tattered sails.

"C'mon, Let's go find him."

I marched toward the side of the ship and could tell Charlie didn't think that was such a grand idea, but he shrugged and followed me to one of the gangplanks. The water foamed below with lamp oil splotching rainbows across the surface.

"Careful," Charlie replied as I stepped up on the wooden plank, spreading my arms like seagulls swarming the bow of the boat as chum was being tossed into the water. Carefully, I began making my way over to Bonnet's ship.

I gulped and tried to push the thoughts of what kind of monsters might lurk beneath the wake. Luckily, I managed to keep my balance, avoiding a plummet into the choppy harbor. I turned and watched as Charlie shimmied across.

For once, I was glad for all the commotion because no one paid much attention to us. I laughed at his shuffle, which was kind of penguin-esque. Charlie shot me a scowl, but he kept his trap shut and shuffled across.

We made our way to the stern of the ship, and I still saw no sign of Grandpa, only the hustle of zamboids and the flutter of the sails and the spray of the ocean.

"Let's go," I pointed to an open hatch.

Charlie grumbled something about chronic claustrophobia or seasickness but followed behind me as I grabbed hold of the ladder and headed down into the dark pit of the ship. It was a ten-foot climb down into the bowels of hell and it was stiflingly cold and wet, as if the sea were leaking in. Flickering wax candles sent our shadows crawling across the wooden walls.

"Should've worn thicker socks," Charlie shuddered above me.

I shivered in agreement. It was frigid. At the bottom, we were slapped with the most horrific of smells, a punch in the gut. I held back a gag. Charlie not so much.

The galley of the ship stank like rancid meat, vats of oil, rotting wood, wet socks and a host of other indescribable but truly awful smells. In the sunlight that seeped through the gaps in the slats of wood, I could tell Charlie was a shade in between gray and green. It was dark and there was junk strewn everywhere. Pots, pans, bed rolls, pipes, liquor bottles and an inordinate amount of pirate-type trash. Pelts of some kind of mystery fur. Bear, maybe beaver? Chests filled with tattered coats and boots.

"Holy Toledo! Look over there." I exclaimed. Two goats were eating slop off the floor. "How could anyone stand to live in this pigsty?"

"Maybe you should say goat-sty?" Charlie replied.

"Ha. Ha. Very funny."

We made our way through the galley back toward the bow of the ship occasionally having to step over a hopefully drunk, not dead zamboid pirate. As we got closer to the bow there was a solid wall separating the ship's galley. It had a small door that we opened and stepped through, emerging into what seemed like an entirely different ship.

The darkness and stench from the crew's galley dissipated significantly. This side of the ship had clean, magnificently stained oak hardwood floors. There was no refuse or passed out zamboids and oil lamps lit up the hold displaying a number of private rooms. Lavish velvet curtains, exquisite art and crystal chandeliers filled the room.

I turned to Charlie. "He's got to be in one of these rooms." I didn't want to face the fact that in Dark Charleston, Grandpa Joe may have morphed into a zamboid, guzzling beer from a pewter mug.

"Or were being hoodwinked," Charlie responded back.

The first door was locked. I knocked and called out grandpa's name. No one answered. We moved to the second room. This time the door opened into an empty room.

The third room was stacked floor to ceiling with chests of all shapes and sizes affixed with gold padlocks, their complementary keys mounted on the wall. I guess if I was curious, I would have taken a peek, but I didn't even want to know what the chests contained. I just wanted to find Grandpa Joe and hightail back to my Charleston.

The next door opened into a room that was the exact replica of the room at Fort Moultrie that had transported us here except there was no ham radio. I quickly slammed the door shut trying not to tempt fate and moved to the last door.

The door opened into a small room that contained a bed, a table and a small porcelain washbowl. Bookcases lined the walls and there were fine, delicate paintings scattered across the remaining wall space and even a small ivory piano.

There was a person sitting at a small desk with their back turned. He wore a white linen shirt and pressed pants. The man marked a page in his book and slowly turned around. A small smile followed by a shocked grimace fell across my grandfather's face.

"Alex." He stood up and walked over. He hugged me tightly. Then he looked over at Charlie with a disapproving expression. "I can't believe you brought her here."

"There was no other choice," Charlie interjected. "That demented cowboy, Dalton, figured out a way to cross over to our world. He highjacked us at gun point. There was nothing I could do about it."

"I guess this is all my fault," Grandpa relented. He patted me on the shoulder, and I noticed that he looked older than I had remembered. "I should have never let things get so out of hand. I'm so sorry, Alex. I never wanted this for you."

"Wanted what for me?"

"This madness. You deserve to have a normal life. You need to go to college and study to become a doctor. Contribute something to society."

For the first time in my life, I felt myself getting angry at my grandfather and curtly replied, "You disappeared, vanished. Everyone from my parents and Grandma to the sheriff acted as if it was no big deal. No one even seemed to care. I read your files. I heard you calling out for help on the ham radio. What would you have liked me to do? Just leave you. Go on with life like you never existed."

Grandpa took a deep breath. "I'm sorry. I should have planned for this eventuality."

"Too late for that," I replied staring into the darkness through the porthole.

"Yes, I know. And as you have now discovered the world, or rather, our world is not as it seems."

An explosion boomed in the distance and the ship shook from side to side.

"What was that?" Charlie yelled, as books toppled off the shelf.

Grandpa Joe steadied himself with a hand on the bedframe. "Sounds like a cannon fire. Let's get to the upper deck."

We followed Grandpa back through the galley, noses plugged, and climbed up to the main deck. Pirates were scurrying everywhere trying to untether the ships. It was complete madness. In the distance, I could see a dark cloud of smoke billowing toward us.

Blackbeard came running up to us. He looked disheveled, peering through an ornate spyglass. "We're under attack."

"By whom?" Charlie asked.

"Who do you think, lad. Poe and the bloody British."

"I thought you said they wouldn't be here for at least two more days."

"Well, it appears I got bad information. Because as you can see, they are here. No matter, we will still prevail."

Blackbeard ran off yelling orders to the crew, leaving us to contemplate our fate. I squinted off into the horizon, following the trail of smoke to a single point, and that's when I saw it. A fleet of ships. The largest ship out in front like a slow-moving stampede. But that wasn't what was most impressive, no, it was the large onyx flag mounted to the stern, at least 15 feet across in both directions. Embroidered with pearl thread, a raven: wings spread.

"What are we going to do now?" Charlie yelled to us.

I stared at the warships steaming straight for us with a sense of dread. *This is not good* I thought just as a cannon ball came flying through the air like a meteor striking Vlad's ship dead on. In a flash of fire, splintered wood, and bodies spinning through the air like rag dolls the ship's mast collapsed, toppling over the way a tree falls to a chainsaw.

I should have peed my pants or had a panic attack or curled up in a ball. Instead, a sudden calmness took hold of my mind and body. Maybe it was the realization there were no choices, there were no options. Our fates were set no matter what we did.

The air smelled of burned wood and oil. Plumes of smoke rose gracefully from Vlad's boat. Everyone was quiet.

Then, chaos.

Blackbeard's zamboid crew managed to get the ships separated and tacked forward to face the oncoming warships. We tried to stay out of the way.

I watched Charlie run over to a bin and grab muskets and a sword. "Here," he handed the muskets to us and kept one along with the sword.

"What the heck do I do with this?" I asked, staring down at the pistol.

"For protection," Charlie answered. "Point and fire."

If the situation weren't so dire, I would have laughed after he said that because he fumbled with the gun, obviously unsure how to operate it.

Then a volley of explosions erupted everywhere. It sounded like hell on earth as both sides started unleashing waves of cannonball fire.

The cannon balls looked like round black birds flying through the air, until they got close. Then they looked like destruction. The cannon volley came up short hitting the water, causing a wave of seawater to wash onto the deck. The crew alternated between firing and bailing the water out of the ship. With the deafening noise and the lack of visibility due to smoke it was pure chaos. We stood at the far deck watching as the ships drew closer. Positioned in front of our ship were Stede Bonnet's and Vlad's ships. They were taking the brunt of the attack.

"Oh no," Grandpa exclaimed.

"What?" I shouted.

Grandpa pointed to the nearest British warship. "I think they are going to ram Vlad's ship."

We watched as the warship gained speed as a heavy gust of wind propelled the sails and took center aim on Stede Bonnet's ship, The Adventure. I put my hand across my eyes because I didn't want to watch the ensuing disaster, but that didn't stop me from peeking.

With a deafening crunch the British warship slammed straight into The Adventure. Sailors on both sides were thrown everywhere and screams of terror and agony echoed over the cannon and pistol fire.

Nets flew from the British warship over to Bonnet's and we watched as the British soldiers began steaming across. A hail of musket shots and swords greeted their arrival.

Bonnet had the defensive advantage, but the British had the numbers and for every British sailor cut down one managed to make it across. The battle quickly turned into hand-to-hand combat. Bodies were flung into the ocean. Men struggled to stay afloat; many sank. There was nothing we could do but stand and stare as the British quickly gained the upper hand and Blackbeard's few remaining men jumped overboard rather than risk being cut to shreds.

Blackbeard casually walked over to us like he was taking a Sunday stroll in a park. He pointed to the British warship. "Look at those fools."

We watched as the victorious soldiers, including Lieutenant Maynard, celebrated their apparent victory by jumping up and down, laughing and hurling insults over to us.

"What are we going to do now?" Grandpa asked Blackbeard.

Blackbeard smiled and stroked his chin. "Watch. This is going to be fun."

Before I could ask Blackbeard what he was talking about in a deafening flash The Adventure blew to smithereens.

The shockwave from the blast threw me down. I covered my head as debris rained down on us, fireballs and flaming planks of wood. Then I watched as a giant wave hit the ship like a tsunami. The ship rolled from side to side sending us up and down and up and down. Luckily, we weren't injured and slowly we stood to evaluate the carnage. Maynard's ship had been obliterated from existence. Nothing stirred.

Blackbeard let out a huge bellow and shook his fist to the sky. "By Lord I got you this time Maynard. I knew that's exactly what that silly fool was going to do. He is so predictable. I packed The Adventure's entire cargo hold with explosives."

"How did the explosives ignite?" Charlie asked.

"I had a zamboid down in the hold. He set the fuses."

"How in the world did he know when to set off the explosives?" Charlie asked.

"Easy. I told the dumb bastard if the ship was rammed to count to 100 and then light it up. Which in hindsight was not too smart of me because I'm not sure if zamboids can even count that high. But no matter because as you can see my plan worked splendidly."

"But what about that poor guy?" I asked.

"Poor guy. It's a zamboid! Anyway, you should thank me Miss Alex. You know who I stuck down there?"

"No."

"He was after my time in your world but I'm sure you've heard of Jack the Ripper."

"Yes, I have," I answered. "But how did he end of up here?"

"Like everything else. From that demented crackpot Poe. I didn't know about Ripper's reputation, but I guess Poe had had enough of him because he sent him to me to serve on my ship. But the person you can actually blame for his presence is your grandfather."

"What do you mean by that?" I said defensively.

"He's right," Grandfather interjected. "I told Poe the story of Jack the Ripper one night, but I had no idea Poe would reincarnate him here as a zamboid."

"Not only that but Mr. Ripper had also taken quite an interest in you, Miss Alex. In fact, if it wasn't for my keen eye the other night, things might be a whole lot different for you right now."

"What do you mean?" I asked suddenly feeling queasy.

"Mr. Ripper seemed to have taken quite a shine to you. He had been stalking you ever since she boarded the ship."

"That must have been the pirate I told you was watching me," I said to Charlie.

"Yes, it was. Just because this is a different world doesn't mean that it changes your true nature. Your essence, your soul transcends worlds. And upon seeing a young lady like Miss Alex, well let's say, Ripper's natural instincts set in. He wasn't going to stop until he had sliced her open. Of course, I was never going to let that happen so when I got the chance I clobbered him over the head and tied him up to make sure she was safe. I then transferred him over to The Adventure and told him that if he did what I requested, I'd give you to him. Which, of course, I wasn't going to do, but zamboids are really dumb."

Even though I was more than a little irritated about being used as bait, Blackbeard had protected me. "I guess I owe you a big thank you."

Blackbeard bowed, dipped his ornate hat and replied, "At your service. So, we all agree Ripper got what he deserved."

No of us put up an argument. And anyway, there was still a battle to win or lose.

"They're moving on to Vlad's," Grandpa yelled over the commotion. "If they take his ship then it's just us."

"What should we do?" I asked.

"Poe wants to know the future," Grandpa replied. "He wants to use me to learn about all the horrors of the modern world to help create this world. He isn't interested in any of the accomplishments, he only wants to hear about destruction and evil."

"Should we jump and try to swim for it?" Charlie asked desperately.

"We'll never make it," I answered back. "The shore is too far, and the current is way too strong."

"Okay, here is the plan," Grandpa interjected. "If Poe takes Vlad's ship and things are looking bad here, I will surrender directly to Poe. I will make a deal with him that I will go and work for him, if he lets you two go free and return home."

"But we can't leave you here," I pleaded.

Grandpa grabbed my shoulders and looked me in the eye. "That is the way it will be, no negotiations! This was my choice to come here, not yours. You have a future in our world, but not here. Here, there would only be misery. I couldn't live with myself if you were forced to do Poe's bidding. I have something he wants, and I think he will agree to the terms if it comes to that."

I started to argue but I knew he was right, and I could never change his mind. Blackbeard's stunt slowed but didn't stop Poe or the British who now appeared to have seized control of Vlad's ship. The situation was growing bleaker by the second when we saw a man swimming toward our ship. It was Vlad who had somehow survived the carnage. We ran over and pulled him out of the waters, half-drowned, by Blackbeard's crew.

We went over to assess the situation and ran into Blackbeard and Vlad having a heated argument. I looked out at the British warships with a sense of foreboding. They had tacked and were slowly approaching with Poe's ship staying well behind, letting the British do the dirty work and obviously keeping out of harm's way.

"Damn you Vlad, there is no time left," Blackbeard cursed. "Time to unleash the demons!"

Vlad looked out at the approaching warships and replied stoically, "I think you're right."

"What's the plan?" I yelled to Blackbeard.

He gave us a wry smile. "This is my last move but I'm not sure if it will be checkmate for them or for us."

Vlad closed his eyes and his face started contorting like he was having the worst nightmare of all time. He opened his eyes and proclaimed, "It is done."

There was an eerie silence, as if the world had paused for a brief moment and then I heard Charlie call out, "Look, over there."

We turned and at first all I could see was what looked like a black cloud moving low across the horizon toward us.

"What in dear lord is that?" Grandpa asked.

Blackbeard gave us a wry smile. "Vlad has an army of gargoyles and griffins. He has trained these monsters to carry explosives and the plan is for them to fly overhead and bombard the British warships. Well, that is the plan in theory."

"Easier said than done," Vlad interjected. "You remember the training runs. Half of the time they dropped the dummy explosives on us. This is a last resort that could spell our doom by our own hands. We'd better pray."

"Pray? This is the contingency plan?" Charlie asked incredulously.

Blackbeard turned to us. "Best take cover. Things are about to get a bit dicey. Those stupid birds are dumb as rocks."

I turned and saw the flock of gruesome looking gargoyles and griffins getting closer and closer. There were hundreds of them, and they were clutching cylinders in their talons. Great, I never thought my demise would be being blown to smithereens by flying monsters aboard Blackbeard's pirate ship while fighting Edgar Allen Poe in a place called Dark Charleston.

The black shadow of death flew over our ship, and I swear the temperature dropped twenty degrees. There was a series of loud explosions and a huge fireball, followed by a rush of salt water that crashed down on us.

I closed my eyes and held my breath. Explosions and screams reverberated all around and it seemed as if time had slowed even though I knew only a minute or two had passed.

Just when I thought I couldn't take it any longer, screams of delight made me open my eyes. Blackbeard and Vlad were locked arm-in-arm dancing around in a circle.

"By gosh, you crazy vampire, it worked." Blackbeard yelled. They hugged while clapping each other on the back and the zamboid pirates started singing a sea shanty.

I stared at the flailing British warship. It was a smoldering mess of destruction and was quickly sinking into the harbor.

I hated to interrupt everyone's celebration, but I thought they had forgotten something. "What about Poe?" I called out to Blackbeard.

His ship had turned 180 degrees and was heading back out of the harbor as fast as the wind could carry it. Poe was fleeing. The raven shrinking in the horizon.

"The heck with him," Blackbeard answered. "There are forces moving upon him as we speak. We'll let them do the rest of the dirty work. It is time for us to celebrate! Rum anyone?"

CHAPTER 16

GOODBYE
DARK CHARLESTON

The celebration aboard the Queen Anne's Revenge lasted late into the night. Drunken shenanigans abound with barrels of rum and beer and explosions from muskets being fired into the air. In the midst of the jubilation a feast magically appeared with breads, shrimp, fish, lamb, fruits and exotic delicacies served to all including the zamboids. At some point during the festivities, we snuck away taking shelter in Grandpa's cabin to try and get some sleep.

Despite the raucous celebration I drifted off to sleep dreaming about how great it would feel to be home again and not in the gelatinous belly of Dark Charleston.

At sunrise we left our cabins sidestepping sleeping zamboids. We headed up on deck where a red sun rose gracefully over the horizon, casting a bloody glow on the water, reminiscent of yesterday's battle.

"Wow, and I thought I had fun last night. Look at those two," Charlie pointed to a disheveled Vlad and Blackbeard who were lying upon bundles of ropes smoking pipes, passing a jug of rum between them. Pluto was lazily laying in between them with a satisfied sly look on its face.

"I heard that," Blackbeard bellowed glancing our way. "Life is short my friends. Every day should be a celebration."

"That's true," Charlie responded. "And Mr. Vlad, do you think I can get your honey mead recipe before we leave?"

Vlad rose a finger in consideration, but before he could answer Grandpa interjected, "When are we heading back to Fort Moultrie?"

Blackbeard took another swig from the jug, burped, and answered, "I'll give these zamboids one more hour and then we'll head out. It is time to return you home before Poe gets anymore wise ideas and tries to highjack you again."

Blackbeard and Vlad rose unstably, bracing themselves against the side of the ship, and started rustling up the hungover zamboids to prepare for departure.

Pluto walked over to us. The cat looked like it had gained a few pounds. "We'll you seem to be quite content aboard this ship."

"Yes. It is much better than Poe's castle and his torturous ways. I have fresh air, the zamboids leave me alone and there is an endless bounty of delicacies to choose from. What right-minded feline wouldn't be in heaven in such a place?"

"We have to go back home."

"Yes, I know," Pluto meowed.

"I made you a promise," I continued. "You know I would take you back to my Charleston if I could, but I'm not sure you would survive the passage."

Pluto looked up at me. "You've kept your promise, Miss Alex. You saved me and I will always be grateful. Blackbeard has taken a shine to me, even if he won't admit it. He lets me sleep in his quarters with him and he has requested I stay aboard as the ship's official mascot."

I picked Pluto up and gave him a big hug just as Blackbeard appeared beside us with his spyglass. He barked orders at the zamboids and conversed eloquently with Vlad about sea currents and battle tactics, reminiscing on yesterday's events. We had a few days sailing left so now was the opportunity to further my discussion with Grandpa about, well, everything.

We settled in for the voyage and made space for ourselves out of the way near the stern of the ship. The ocean spray was refreshing and oddly warm. Hopefully in a few days we'll be back to the Charleston Harbor I knew. The one framed with antebellum houses and gothic churches and sweet gum trees. Where cannons were merely artifacts of the past, a distant recollection of battles printed in high school textbooks. We sailed out of Ocracoke Inlet into open seas, and now was the time for some answers.

"Okay Grandpa, you answered a few of my questions but you have not given me the full story."

"You're right. Ask me anything you want."

"First off, what is the deal with the sheriff?"

"That is hard to answer."

"Really?" I exclaimed, thinking this was going to be harder than pulling teeth. I mean, we were currently sailing on a 300- year-old ship in an alternate world molded from the dark depths of Edgar Allen Poe's brain. This warranted some elaboration.

Grandpa sighed and took a deep breath. "The sheriff. That is a bit complicated, but I guess this will explain a lot of things. In our physical universe there is matter and anti-matter. Forces and anti-forces. On earth there is good and evil. As you have now learned there are infinite universes, multiverses and other realms of existence. Some are remarkably similar to ours, others that are incomprehensible. In our realm there are two major underlying opposing forces. One is The Light and the other is The Shadow. Wherever there is The Light, there is The Shadow. These are the fundamental forces of existence. Although they are contradictory by nature, they are bound together on a cosmic scale. Simply put, one cannot exist without the other. In our realm, The Light seeks to maintain order, while The Shadow seeks chaos and thrives on doubt and survival logic."

"So, is it something like The Light is good and The Shadow is evil?" I asked.

"Not necessarily. There can be terrible order and transformative, positive chaos. It is still a learning process even for me but the best way I can describe it is that this isn't about black and white but many, many shades of grey."

"Okay but what does this have to do with you and the sheriff."

"I'm sure Charlie told you about the mysteries and unusual circumstances of the 33rd parallel and that we are geographically located on something called the bloodlines of Earth."

"Yes."

"The Light and The Shadow dwell in realms outside of the existence of our reality, in a place called The Void. The Void is beautiful and heavenly for some and a terrible hell for others. The simple answer to your question is that I have become part of The Light and The Sheriff is part of The Shadow. We help maintain the balance between the two."

"Were you chosen or something?"

Grandpa smiled. "Not exactly. We are but an inestimably tiny part of this on the grand scale. But every person plays a role and their existence matters. Everyone is born with a little part of The Shadow and a little part of The Light imbedded in their essence or soul. What the sheriff and I have in common is that we are searchers or explorers, and our searches eventually led us to make a choice to be involved."

"What we're y'all searching for? I don't understand the connection."

"For me, my search led to The Ford Files which took me down the path of a realization that the world we see, that we experience in our day-to-day lives, is not everything. The best way to describe my position is a quote by Einstein. He said—

"*We are in the position of a little child entering a huge library, whose walls are covered to the ceiling with books in many different languages. The child knows that someone must have written those books. It does not know who or how. It does not understand the languages in which they are written. The child notes a definite plan in the arrangement of the books, a mysterious order, which it does not comprehend but only dimly suspects.*"

"In regard to the mysteries of the universe it's like we are all children searching, trying to learn the language so we can then begin to read the books. Does this make any sense?"

"A little, I guess."

"And to answer your question about being chosen, no one rings a bell. There is not a ceremony or a secret club or some membership. Every person, at some time in their lives, experiences an event. An unexplained event or a feeling or an understanding. Because of life circumstances some people dismiss it, some push it back deep into their consciousness, some even just forget. But for some, it changes them forever. When it changes a person forever, they search. And inevitably that search leads them to The Light and The Shadow. And then to choose between the two."

"Is that why you said you never wanted this for me?"

"Yes. Because I know you and you won't pretend like this never happened."

"Unless someone slipped me the most powerful dose of LSD in the world, I think all this would be pretty hard to forget about."

Grandpa laughed. "I know. But I'll make you a deal."

"Okay. I'm listening?"

"Go to college and become a doctor. The world needs doctors and nurses. You can contribute something to society."

"What kind of a deal is that?"

"In return, I will open the Ford Files to you. And in your spare time, I will include you in my searching and exploration and I will also pass along everything I have discovered. Then you can choose for yourself to follow either The Light or The Shadow."

I thought about it for a minute and Grandpa did have a good point. Why couldn't I do both? I mean, in terms of my life I could make my own rules, right? Although the combination felt a little ironic. On one hand, there was the empirical nature of medicine, disease is disease. On the other, there was ghost-hunting and alternate dimensions, which, if I tried to explain to anyone, would lead me to institutionalization of some sorts and strong antipsychotic medication.

I held out my hand. "It's a deal about med school but I've already made my choice regarding The Light or The Shadow."

We shook hands. Grandpa looked resigned but also pleased.

"Do you think the sheriff was trying to trap you in Dark Charleston?"

"I don't think so. But since he has much different objectives than I do his actions can sometimes be baffling. I think he was trying to find a way to cross over to this world and I just beat him to it."

"What would he hope to accomplish by coming here?" I asked.

"Remember, we are both explorers. What binds us together despite our differences is the quest for knowledge and discovery. Poe's wanted to create a new world skewed toward The Shadow, tipping the scale so to speak."

"How many people are involved in this?" I continued with my questions.

"I have no idea." Grandpa answered. "Again, there is no formal membership to my knowledge, although people who dedicate themselves to The Light or The Shadow tend to attract each other."

"Are there others in Charleston besides you and the sheriff?"

"Of course, and when our paths cross, we tend to know it and that is how I met Charlie."

I looked over at Charlie who had a big grin on his face. Geez, he was smug son-of-a-gun. I knew he had some sort of superiority complex the way he held his knowledge over my head like a professor wore tweed.

"Oh no, don't tell me you're in this as well?" I asked.

He winked. "Welcome to the club Alex."

I suppressed a groan.

Charlie pointed up to the sky. "What is that?"

We looked and rapidly approaching the ship was a large black bird. "I think it is a raven," I answered.

"What is it carrying?" Charlie asked.

"Maybe it is a message," Grandpa interjected. "Like a messenger pigeon."

The raven flew overhead, and a scroll dropped from its talons right in front of us. I picked it up and unrolled the parchment.

"It's from Poe," I replied.

"Well, go ahead and read it," Charlie directed.

My Friends,

I send you greetings and congratulations on your grand victory at Ocracoke Inlet. For now, I bid you farewell with my story:

Lo! Death reared himself a throne and left me in a strange city where I found myself lying alone. Upon seeing this I fell into a great rage, without exactly knowing why.

But I awoke one morning and my rage was gone, my soul was at peace. I realized I didn't need a story; I didn't need a real world. I just had to keep dreaming. And I became the stories, I became the places.' I was the lights, the deserts, the faraway worlds. We were here before you even existed.

I know you call me mad; but the question is not yet settled, whether madness is or is not the loftiest intelligence. You think of me as a foe, I think of you as a friend.

I created this world for the few who love me and whom I love—to those who feel rather than to those who think—to the dreamers and those who put faith in dreams as in the only realities because all that we see or seem is but a dream within a dream. Never forget my little playthings; the pen is mightier than the sword.

Farewell and safe travels, 'till our paths inevitably cross again my good friends.

- Edgar Allen Poe

CHAPTER 17

AN ENDING

We sailed uneventfully back to the Vlad's castle with no sign of Poe or thankfully any new conjuring he might have written into existence. The harbor emerged like a shadow, a memory of Dark Charleston. I missed the normalcy of the open sea, or at least as normal as sailing on a pirate ship could be.

The castle, still grand and definitely haunted, stood like a pillar of the macabre, its stone façade etched out of something other than time. The water shallowed and the ship set anchor.

Blackbeard extended a hand as I made my way down into the rowboat. We were escorted to shore along with Blackbeard and Vlad, who planned on accompanying us to Fort Moultrie. They shared banter about their glorious victory. We hit the beach and a zamboid heaved it onto the sand.

Without delay we hiked back to the fort with Blackbeard and Vlad. Back across sand and beach shrubbery, the harbor churning like a reminder of the past few days. As we approached the outer wall I stopped dead in my tracks. My heart skipped a beat because standing outside the fort was Dalton, with one of Poe's monks who was sitting at a wooden writing desk staring off into the distance.

Dalton had a senile frown and his greasy hair tied into a slick ponytail. His eyes gleamed murderously, and he drank from a flask.

Charlie whipped around toward Blackbeard, pushing an accusatory finger in the pirate's face. "What is this?" Charlie shouted to Blackbeard. "Is this a set up?"

"I may be a pirate, but I keep my word. This is the last bit of business we have to deal with before you go back to Charleston. Your grandfather will understand."

I looked over at Grandpa Joe who shook his head in agreement. "It is okay. We're good," he said trying to relieve our apprehension.

I gave Dalton my biggest side eye which he returned. He rose from his seated position and capped the flask, wiping his lips with the back of his hand.

"Dalton is one of Poe's men and he will remain that way after you leave but we are all in agreement," Blackbeard explained. "We want the portal to your world closed for good. If we don't do it here and now who is to stop Poe from bringing someone like your grandpa back to this world? We've tasted your world and call us old-fashioned, but we don't want any part of it. Dalton snatched one of Poe's monks and he is going to write the end of this chapter, closing the connection between our worlds. After you leave, the portal will forever close and what happens here, stays here."

Dalton tipped his hat as we approached. He kicked the monk with his cowboy boot. "Get to writing," he ordered, spitting out a stream of blackish tobacco juice.

The monk, face waxen, started furiously scribbling on the parchment, dipping his quill in and out of a vat of dark red ink. After a few minutes he set his quill down and resumed a catatonic state.

I wanted to wave my hand in front of the poor monk's face, cloudy eyes poised on the horizon, but I thought against it, especially when I spotted Dalton's hand resting on his firearm.

"Is it done?" Blackbeard asked Dalton.

"I don't know how to read," Dalton replied tightening his grip on his pistol.

Vlad was standing next to the table and looked down at the monk's book. "For some reason I have the ability to speak your language, but I can only read my native languages of Latin, Romanian and Hungarian."

"Dear lord," Blackbeard exclaimed. "The burden of education! You know, in their history books, I'm just a murderous sack of flesh, gold-hungry! Unlike you buffoons, I can read!" Vlad looked like he was going to correct Blackbeard, but the pirate pushed him out of the way, stalked around the table and grabbed the monk's book. He began reading:

"The explorers were happy and dauntless and sagacious. They were surrounded by buffoons, there were improvisatori, there were zamboids, there were musicians, there was Beauty, there was wine. All this lay within Poe's World. In an assembly of phantasms such as I have painted, it may well be supposed that no ordinary appearance could have excited such sensation. As we find cycle within cycle without end, space itself is infinite; for there may be an infinity of matter to fill it. Yet all revolving around one far-distant centre which is the God-Poe. But there must be a boundary to this realm which cannot be crossed. And in that end this boundary shall close once these explorers pass through, never to return."

"That's very Poe-etic ending," I replied.

Blackbeard winked at me then burst into laughter. Everyone joined in, except Dalton who took another swig from his flask.

Blackbeard gave me a big bear hug. "Good-bye, Miss Alex."

"Bye," I said, suddenly feeling very nostalgic. "Take good care of Pluto."

Blackbeard gave me a smile. "Of course."

Vlad bowed. "Please, when you get back to your home can you contact your historians and see that they make the proper corrections to my legacy?" Vlad requested.

"Oh boy, he never stops!" Blackbeard laughed.

"Few men's names are known to the world generations after they depart. You are one of a few Vlad. We will gladly tell everyone we know about your bravery, the love you have for your people, and your real historic achievements."

Vlad clasped his hands together and bowed pleased with my response.

We walked into the fort, down to the room. With no hesitation Grandpa opened the door and a brilliant light streamed out. I couldn't even see inside the room the light was so intense. I shielded my eyes with the back of my hand and followed Grandpa and Charlie into the room. It smelled mostly of dust and old age, but the faintest whiffs of marsh and salt emanated from the back as if the light itself was a neuron connecting the two Charleston's. Like a live wire, pulsing with electricity.

A blinding light encompassed us followed by a swooshing noise. Then we were gone but not really. Yet, I knew Dark Charleston was gone, the way an apparition is quick to appear and quicker to disappear.

We stepped outside the room and walked down the tunnel out into the fort's courtyard. When I turned back around, the tunnel had disappeared, evaporating like a fine mist. Though the memory of Dark Charleston was stark, I felt it too would eventually do the same. As if some facet of Poe's magic had worked itself into my brain and fogged it, carrying away its memory.

Charlie, Grandpa, and I exited the fort, and I looked up to the blue sky and spotted a plane flying high overhead. Yep, we were back home.

A sign posted: "Historic Monument." Charleston. Crumbling bricks. Paved roads. A car. Cookie cutter beach bungalows. The faint beacon of a cargo ship offshore.

Charlie stared back at the fort, and I nudged him in the ribs. "No. We're not even going to look."

"But why?" He asked.

"Because it is Blackbeard's treasure. We made a promise. A gentleman's agreement. He trusted us and don't forget he kept his end of the bargain. Without him we would never have gotten back home. It would be bad karma."

"But what about my Riverdogs season tickets?" Charlie protested.

I glared at him, "Seriously?"

"I'll take you to as many games as you want," Grandpa interceded.

"All right. And since Alex is now in the club, I thought the three of us could reinvestigate the Boo Hag creature up in the Francis Marion swamp."

"I'm in," I added.

Grandpa gave me a look mixed with exasperation and amusement, but mostly resignation. He knew The Ford Files was part of my life now.

I gave Charlie a fist bump.

Exhaustion started to set in as we trudged to the fort's exit. The sun rose warmly over the horizon, a reminder of the blistering heat of August.

We walked out of the fort and to my surprise, a police car was parked outside. The sheriff leaned up against the passenger door. He had his reflector sunglasses on and a toothpick dangling from his mouth with his trademark smirk on his face. I hope this wasn't trouble.

"Welcome home, Joe," the sheriff called out. "How was Dark Charleston?"

"Interesting."

"You'll have to tell me about it one of these days."

"Absolutely."

The sheriff turned to me. He took the toothpick out of his mouth and pointed at me and said in an amused way, "I understand you have chosen to be part of The Light?"

I didn't understand how he could have known that, but then again, like Einstein's quote I too was just an awe-stricken child in an endless library with no comprehension of the mysterious forces in the universe.

The sheriff threw the toothpick onto the ground. "Well, that is that. I guess y'all need a ride home?"

"That would be great," Grandpa replied.

The sheriff walked around to the driver's side of the vehicle, put his arms up on the hood of the car, and looked over at Grandpa. He made that strange clicking noise in his throat and then said nonchalantly, "Oh yeah, Joe. There is one more thing, your wife has gone missing."

KA-POW!

Made in USA - Kendallville, IN
31874_9798335357845
12.13.2024 2107